113 MINUTES

JAMES PATTERSON is one of the best-known and biggest-selling writers of all time. His books have sold in excess of 325 million copies worldwide and he has been the most borrowed author in UK libraries for the past nine years in a row. He is the author of some of the most popular series of the past two decades – the Alex Cross, Women's Murder Club, Detective Michael Bennett and Private novels – and he has written many other number one bestsellers including romance novels and stand-alone thrillers.

James is passionate about encouraging children to read. Inspired by his own son who was a reluctant reader, he also writes a range of books for young readers including the Middle School, I Funny, Treasure Hunters, House of Robots, Confessions and Maximum Ride series. James is the proud sponsor of the World Book Day Award and has donated millions in grants to independent bookshops. He lives in Florida with his wife and son.

BOOK**SHOTS**

STORIES AT THE SPEED OF LIFE

What you are holding in your hands right now is no ordinary book, it's a BookShot.

BookShots are page-turning stories by James Patterson and other writers that can be read in one sitting.

Each and every one is fast-paced, 100% story-driven; a shot of pure entertainment guaranteed to satisfy.

Available as new, compact paperbacks, ebooks and audio, everywhere books are sold.

BookShots – the ultimate form of storytelling. From the ultimate storyteller.

113 MINUTES

JAMES PATTERSON

WITH *MAX DILALLO*

BOOK**SHOTS**

1 3 5 7 9 10 8 6 4 2

BookShots
20 Vauxhall Bridge Road
London SW1V 2SA

BookShots is part of the Penguin Random House
group of companies whose addresses can be found at
global.penguinrandomhouse.com

Penguin
Random House
UK

First published by BookShots in 2016

www.penguin.co.uk

A CIP catalogue record for this book is available from the British Library.

ISBN 9781786530417

Printed and bound in Great Britain by Clays Ltd, St Ives Plc

MIX
Paper from
responsible sources
FSC® C018179

Penguin Random House is committed to a sustainable future
for our business, our readers and our planet. This book is made
from Forest Stewardship Council® certified paper.

113 MINUTES

3 MINUTES, 10 SECONDS

A MOTHER'S INSTINCT to protect her child—the most powerful force on the planet.

Right now I'm bursting with it. Overwhelmed by it. Trembling from it.

My son, my precious little boy, is hurt. Or, God forbid, it's worse.

I don't know the details of what's happened. I don't even know where he is.

I just know I have to save him.

I slam on the brakes. The tires of my old Dodge Ram screech like hell. One of them pops the curb, jerking me forward hard against the wheel. But I'm so numb with fear and panic, I barely feel the impact.

I grab the door handle—but stop and count to three. I force myself to take three deep breaths. I make the sign of the cross: three times again.

And I pray that I find my son fast—*in three minutes or less.*

I leap out and start running. The fastest I've ever moved in my life.

Oh, Alex. What have you done?

He's such a good kid. Such a smart kid. A tough kid, too—especially with all our family's been going through. I'm not a perfect mother. But I've always done the best I know how. Alex isn't perfect, either, but I love him more than anything. And I'm so proud of him, so proud of the young man he's becoming before my eyes.

I just want to see him again—*safe*. And I'd give anything for it. *Anything*.

I reach the two-story brick building's front doors. Above them hangs a faded green-and-white banner I must have read a thousand times:

HOBART HIGH SCHOOL—HOME OF THE RAIDERS

Could be any other high school in America. Certainly any in sweltering west Texas. But somewhere inside is my son. And goddamnit, I'm coming for him.

I burst through the doors—*But where the hell am I going?*

I've spent more hours in this building than I could ever count. Hell, I graduated from this school nearly twenty years ago. But suddenly, the layout feels strange to me. Foreign.

I start running down the central hallway. Terrified. Desperate. Frenzied.

Oh, Alex. At fifteen, he's still just a child. He loves comic books—especially the classics like Batman and Spider-Man. He loves video games, the more frenzied the better. He loves being outdoors, too. Shooting and fishing especially. Riding his dirt bike—shiny blue, his favorite color—around abandoned oil fields with his friends.

But my son is also turning into an adult. He's been staying out later and later, especially on Fridays and Saturdays. He's started cruising around the county in his friends' cars. Just a few weeks ago—I didn't say anything, I was too shocked—but I smelled beer on his breath. The teenage years can be so hard. I remember my own rocky ones. I just hope I've raised him well enough to handle them....

"Alex!" I scream, my shrill voice echoing off the rows of metal lockers.

The text had come from Alex's cell phone—Miss Molly this is Danny—but it was written by his best friend since first grade. I always liked Danny. He came from a good family. But rumor was, he'd recently started making some bad choices. I'd been secretly worrying he'd pressure Alex to make the same ones someday.

The moment I read that text, I knew he had.

Alex did too much. Not breathing. At school come fast.

Next thing I remember, I'm in my truck roaring down Route 84, dialing Alex's cell, cursing when neither of them answers. I call his principal. I call my brothers. I call 911.

And then I pray: I call in a favor from God.

"Alex!" I yell again, even louder, to no one and everyone. "Where are you?!"

But the students I pass now just gawk. Some point and

snicker. Others point and click, snapping cell-phone pictures of the crazy lady running wild through their school.

Don't they know what's happening?! How can they be like this, so…

Wait. Teenagers spread rumors faster than a brushfire, and it's way too quiet. Maybe they *don't* know.

He must be on the second floor.

I head to the nearest stairway and pound up the steps. My lungs start to burn and my heart races. At the top, the hallway forks.

Damn it, which way, where is he?!

Something tells me to hang a left. Maybe a mother's intuition. Maybe blind, stupid luck. Either way, I listen.

There, down at the end, a growing crowd is gathering outside the boys' bathroom. Kids and teachers. Some yelling. Some crying. All panicking.

Like I am.

"I'm his mother!" I push and shove toward the middle. "Move! Out of my way!"

I spot Alex's legs first, splayed out limp and crooked. I see his scuffed-up Converses, the soles wrapped in duct tape, apparently some kind of fashion trend. I recognize the ratty old pair of Levi's he wore at breakfast this morning, the ones I sewed a new patch onto last week. I can make out a colorful rolled-up comic book jutting out of the back pocket.

And then I see his right arm, outstretched on the ground.

His lifeless fingers clutching a small glass pipe, its round tip charred and black.

Oh, Alex, how could you do this?

His homeroom teacher, the school nurse, and a fit youngish man I don't recognize wearing a HHS baseball T-shirt are all hunched over his body, frantically performing CPR.

But *I'm* the one who's just stopped breathing.

"No, no, no…Alex! My poor baby…"

How did this happen? How did I let it? How could I have been so blind?

My knees start to buckle. My head gets light. My vision spins. I start to lose my balance….

"Molly, easy now, we got ya."

I feel four sturdy hands grab me from behind: Stevie and Hank, the best big brothers a girl could ask for. As soon as I called them to say what had happened, they rushed right over to the high school. They're my two rocks. Who I need now more than ever.

"He's gonna be all right," Hank whispers. "Everything's gonna be fine."

I know he's just saying that—but they're words I desperately need to hear and believe. I don't have the strength, or the will, to respond.

I let him and Stevie hold me steady. I can't move a muscle. Can't take my eyes off Alex, either. He looks so thin, so weak. So young. So vulnerable. His skin pale as Xerox paper. His lips flecked with frothy spittle. His eyes like sunken glass orbs.

"Who sold him that shit?!"

Stevie spins to face the crowd, spewing white-hot rage. His voice booms across the hallway. "Who did this?! Who?!"

The crowd instantly falls silent. A retired Marine, Stevie is that damn scary. Not a sound can be heard—except for the wail of an ambulance siren.

"Somebody better talk to me! Now!"

Yet no one makes a peep. No one dares to.

But no one *needs* to.

Because as I watch the last drops of life drain from Alex's body, my own life changed and dimmed forever, I realize I already know the answer.

I know who killed my son.

2 MINUTES, 45 SECONDS

THE OLD JEEP rattles slowly down the long dusty road, like a cheetah stalking its prey. A symphony of crickets fills the hot night air. A passing train whistles off in the distance. A pale sliver of moon, the only light for miles.

Gripping the steering wheel is Stevie Rourke. His eyes gaze straight ahead. A former staff sergeant in the United States Marine Corps, he's forty-four years old, six feet six inches tall, and 249 pounds of solid muscle. A man so loyal to his friends and family, he'd rush the gates of hell for them, and wrestle the devil himself.

Hank Rourke, trim and wiry, younger by only a few years, with a similar devotion but a far shorter fuse, is sitting shotgun—and loading shells into one, too.

"We're less than 180 seconds out," Stevie says.

Hank grunts in understanding.

The two brothers ride in tense silence for the rest of the brief trip. No words needed. They've discussed their plan and know exactly what they're going to do.

Confront the good-for-nothing son of a bitch who killed their fifteen-year-old nephew.

Stevie and Hank both loved that boy. Loved him as if he were their own son. And Alex loved them both back. Molly's worthless drunk of a husband had taken off when the boy was just a baby. But no one had shed any tears. Not then, not since. Molly reclaimed her maiden name for her and Alex. The whole Rourke family was already living together on their big family farm, and with no children of their own, Hank and Stevie stepped right up. The void left by one lousy father was filled by two incredible uncles. And Alex's life was all the better for it.

Until today. When his life came to a heartbreaking end.

Both brothers dropped everything as soon as Molly called them. They drove together straight to the high school, their truck rattling along at over a hundred miles per hour. They were hoping for the best....

But had prepared themselves for the worst.

The doctors and sheriff's department are treating Alex's death as an accident. At least for now. Just two kids being kids, messing with shit they shouldn't have been.

But it was an accident that didn't have to happen.

And somebody is going to pay.

Their destination soon comes into sight: a cluster of low-slung wood and metal buildings that seem to shimmer in the still-scorching desert heat. Hank surveys the area with a pair of forest-green binoculars.

"Don't see anyone on patrol. Maybe we can sneak up on him after all."

Stevie shakes his head.

"That bastard knows we're coming."

The Jeep comes to a stop in front of a rusty padlocked gate on the perimeter of the property, dotted with dry shrubs and scraggly trees. At the end of a short driveway sits a tumble-down little shack.

The man they've come for lives inside.

Stuffing his Glock 19 into his belt behind his back, Stevie steps out of the Jeep first—and the blistering desert air hits him like a semi. Instantly he's flooded with memories of the nighttime covert ops he ran in Desert Storm. But that was a distant land, where more than two decades earlier he served with honor and distinction.

Tonight, he's in Scurry County, Texas. He doesn't have an elite squad to back him up. Only his jumpy little brother.

And the stakes aren't just higher. They're personal.

"Lay a hand on my gate, Rourke, I'll blow it clean off."

Old Abe McKinley is standing on his farmhouse porch, shakily aiming a giant wood-handled Colt Anaconda. With his wild mane of white hair and blackened teeth, he either looks awful for seventy-five, or like total shit for sixty.

But Stevie doesn't scare easy—or back down.

"I want to talk to you, Abe. Nothing more."

"Then tell your baby brother to be smart. And put down his toy."

"If you tell your folks to do the same."

Abe snorts. *Not a chance.*

Stevie shrugs. Worth a try. "Then at least tell 'em," he says, "to quit pretending to hide."

After a reluctant nod from the old man, Hank tosses his pump-action Remington back into the Jeep. Simultaneously, fourteen of McKinley's goons, hidden all around the compound, slowly step out of the shadows. Some were crouched behind bushes. Others, trees. A few were lying prone in the knee-high grass that covers most of McKinley's two dozen acres.

Each man is wearing full hunting camo and a ski mask, and clutching a semiautomatic weapon.

Stevie was right. The bastard sure *did* know they'd be coming around here.

"Now, then." Stevie clears his throat. "As I was saying—"

"Sorry to hear about your sister's boy." McKinley interrupts. Not one for small talk. He spits a thick squirt of tobacco juice into the dirt. "Tragedy."

Stevie swallows his rage at the intentional sign of complete disrespect. "You sound real cut up about it. *About losing a first-time customer.*"

McKinley betrays nothing. "I don't know what you mean by that. If you're implying I had anything to do with—"

Hank's the one who interrupts now. Can't keep his cool like his brother.

"You got four counties hooked on the crystal you cook!"

he shouts, taking a step forward. McKinley's men raise their guns, but Hank doesn't flinch.

"You're the biggest player from here to Lubbock, and everybody knows it. Means one of y'all"—Hank glares at each of the armed men, one by one, their fingers tickling their triggers—"sold our nephew the shit that killed him. Put a live grenade in the hand of a child!"

McKinley just snarls. Then turns and starts heading back inside his house.

"Stevie, Hank, thanks for stopping by. But don't do it again. Or I'll bury you out back with the dogs."

Like a shot from a rifle—*crack!*—the screen door slams shut behind him.

4 MINUTES, 45 SECONDS

TOMORROW MARKS TEN weeks to the day my son Alex died before my eyes.

I can't believe it. It feels like barely ten minutes.

I can still remember so clearly the pair of fresh-faced paramedics who rushed into the hallway and lifted him onto a gurney. I remember the breakneck ambulance ride to the county hospital, all those machines he was hooked up to, clicking and beeping, me clutching his clammy hand, urging him to hang on to his life just as tight.

I remember when we arrived and the EMTs slid out his stretcher, I saw the comic book Alex had in his back pocket. It got jostled and fluttered to the ground. As he was wheeled away into the ER, I stopped to scoop it up, and then frantically ran after them.

I screamed and waved it in the air like a madman, as if they were army medics carrying a blast victim off a battlefield and had left behind his missing limb. Of course I wasn't thinking straight. How could any mother at a time like that? I kept wailing and bawling until finally one of the nurses took hold of those few dozen colorful pages and promised to give them to my son.

"When he wakes up!" I said, both my hands on her shoulders. "Please!"

The nurse nodded. And smiled sadly. "Of course, ma'am. When he wakes up."

Two days later, that crinkled comic book was returned to me.

It came in a sealed plastic bag that also held my son's wallet, cell phone, and the clothes he was wearing when he was admitted, including his Converses wrapped in duct tape and his old pair of Levi's.

Alex never woke up.

My brother Hank suddenly jars me out of my dazed memory—by punching the kitchen wall with his meaty fist so hard, the framed pictures and hanging decorative plates all rattle. He's always been the hotheaded one. The firecracker in the family. Tonight is no different.

"The Rourkes have owned this land for three generations!" he shouts. "No goddamn way we're gonna lose it to the bank in three months!"

Before any of us can respond, he punches the wall again— even harder—and an antique piece of china that belonged to our late grandmother Esther Rourke slips off its holder and smashes into pieces.

Debbie, Hank's bubbly blond wife, gasps in horror. But I

couldn't care less. It's just a thing. An object. Sure, it had been in our family for years, but today our family itself is shattered. My *heart* is shattered. Who cares if some stupid old plate is, too? In fact, I'm happy to clean it up. Happy for a distraction from all the yelling and cursing and arguing of the past hour—which I hope we can wrap up in a few more minutes.

But before I can fetch a broom, Stevie takes my shoulder.

"Walk us through it one more time, Molly," he says. "It's one hell of a plan."

I can't deny that. On the surface, it sounds reckless. Crazy. Nearly impossible.

But I've had plenty of time to think over every last detail. And I believe with every piece of my broken heart that we can do it.

We *have* to do it.

See, well before Alex passed, the bank had been calling—sometimes twice, three times a day. The notices were piling up. Stevie, Hank, their wives, and me, we all scrimped as best we could. Even Alex, my big man, my baby, had been handing over the crumpled five-dollar bills he earned mowing Mrs. Baker's lawn down the road.

But it wasn't enough. The payments, the interest—I knew we'd never be able to cover it all. We'd keep slipping further and further behind. I knew it was only a matter of time before we lost our home for good.

And then, we were faced with a totally unexpected additional expense, which sped the process up even more.

The cost of my only child's funeral.

So now, in just ninety days, the ten-acre farm our family has called home for so long will become the legal property of First Texas Credit Union. Unless we put my "hell of a plan," the one I'd been mulling over for months, into action.

And, by the grace of God, pull it off.

"Save your breath," Hank says to me. "It's madness, Molly. Pure and simple."

Again I can't deny that. At least under normal circumstances, I can't.

"Desperate times," says Stevie's wife, Kim, with a quiet intensity. A military daughter and spouse, she's a wise brunette beauty, no stranger to hard choices. Over the last twelve years that she's been married to my oldest brother, she's become the sister I never had. When it became clear that children of their own weren't in the cards, she could have gotten resentful. Bitter. Instead, Kim directed all that excess love toward Alex. She was the only one of us, for example, who had the patience to teach him to ride a bike, a hobby he kept up until his last days.

"I wanna know what *he* thinks," Hank fires back, pointing at the man who's been sitting in the adjacent dining room, sipping iced sweet tea with lemon, listening patiently this whole time, barely uttering a word. "If *he* says it's crazy, you *know* it's gotta be—"

"Doesn't matter," I say. "This is family-only. Either we're all in, or we're all out. Right on our asses, too."

My brothers and sisters-in-law chew on that. So do Nick

and J.D., two retired Marines Stevie served with in the Middle East so long ago, who became as close as blood. Especially in recent years, they'd become like big brothers to Alex, taking him on hunting and fishing trips for some critical male bonding. They were in the second row at his funeral, two burly ex-soldiers dabbing at their eyes.

I explain one final time exactly what I'm proposing. My plan is a long haul with short odds. It might cost us everything. But doing nothing *definitely* would.

After a tense silence that feels like it goes on forever...

"In," Stevie says simply. Marines don't mince their words.

"Semper fi," says Nick, stepping forward. He and J.D. both give stiff salutes.

Kim clasps her husband's hand. "That makes four, then."

Debbie nervously twirls her yellow locks, blinking, unsure. I like Debbie—or, should I say, I've *grown* to like her. We probably wouldn't be friends if she weren't married to my brother. Debbie's sweet, but timid. Tries a little too hard to please. She'd rather go with the flow than rock the boat, especially when her husband's in it. She looks to Hank for guidance; she doesn't get it. So she does something surprising. She goes with her gut.

"This place, after all these years...it's become *my* home, too. I'll do it."

Hank throws up his hands. He's the final holdout.

"You're asking me to pick my family or my conscience. You understand that?"

My eyes flutter to a framed, faded photograph on the wall of Alex at age six. He's sitting in a tire swing hanging from the branch of a giant oak tree on our farm, smiling a gap-toothed grin. He looks so little. So happy. So innocent.

So alive.

"Sounds like an easy choice to me," I say.

At last, with a heavy sigh, Hank nods. He's in, too.

And so the vote is unanimous. *My plan is a go.*

"Just one little problem," Debbie says nervously, bending down now to pick up the pieces of the antique plate her husband broke.

"Where are we gonna get seventy-five grand to pull this thing off?"

5 MINUTES, 35 SECONDS

IN THE TEN weeks since my son died, I've probably slept less than ten hours.

During the days I'm bone-tired, shuffling from room to room like a zombie. But at night, rest rarely comes. I toss. I turn. I pray. I cry.

My mind keeps replaying my every memory of Alex over and over on a loop. But they're never chronological. They always jump around.

First I might remember watching him when he walked across the stage in his adorable little cap and gown for his kindergarten "graduation" ten years ago.

Then I might think of the joyful look on his face the time he scored a winning goal for his junior-high soccer team.

Then I might see him taking his first tottering steps in the kitchen of our farmhouse.

The same farmhouse my family and I have lived in for decades upon decades.

The same one that could be taken away from us very soon.

Right now I'm lying in bed, sweating through the sheets thanks to the west Texas air, still blasting strong at 1:10 a.m., according to the old clock radio next to my bed.

But I'm not thinking about Alex.

Instead I'm jumpy with nerves. My entire family, nuclear and extended, blood and not, has just agreed to my "hell of a plan." It still hasn't fully sunk in. Tomorrow we start putting it into—

Hang on. I hear something. Outside. A metal *clank,* distant but distinct.

Having been awake most nights for over two months, I've gotten familiar with the sounds at these hours. Like crickets. The occasional coyote howl. Other than that, there *aren't* any sounds. Our farmhouse sits on ten secluded acres.

Maybe it's just an animal. Or maybe…it's an intruder? Or maybe I'm just hearing things, my mind is just playing—

Clank.

There it is again. I have to find out what it is.

I slip out of bed and into some slippers. Then I creep down the hall.

I pad right past the shut door of Alex's room, which I haven't set foot in since the day he died. I don't know when I will again. Maybe never.

I reach Stevie and Kim's bedroom, give the door a knock, then slowly push it open. (They moved back in about two years ago, after Stevie's hours at the oil refinery were cut, to help defray living expenses for all of us.)

Kim is dozing soundly, but next to her is empty space.
Great. He's probably out with Hank, Nick, and J.D., tossing
back a few, something they've been doing more lately to help
numb their grief. But what's the point of having your retired
Marine big brother sleep under the same roof as you if he's not
sleeping there when you need him?

Fine, I'll do it myself.

I tiptoe downstairs and head for the kitchen. I pass
through the doorway, which is "decorated" up and down with
lines marking various Rourke family members' heights over
the years. And not just Alex's. Mine and my brothers'. My late
father, John. My aunt Anna and cousins Matthew and Jacob.
Generations of us.

But I don't have time to be sentimental. Not now.

Not when I'm in danger.

An emergency flashlight sits on top of our old, humming
refrigerator. Wedged behind the fridge is an even older Ruger
bolt-action hunting rifle.

I take both.

I unlock the front door, step outside, flip on the flashlight,
and survey our driveway and front yard. Everything looks
normal. All sounds quiet. I exhale, relieved. Maybe I'm so exhausted, I really am starting to—

Clank.

No, there it is again. I'm sure of it. Coming from *behind*
the farmhouse.

Gripping the flashlight and gun tightly, I slowly stalk

around the side of the house, trying to crunch the dry grass as little as possible so as not to give away my position.

I reach the backyard now, where I haven't been in weeks. No sign of anyone. Not near the house, at least. But then my flashlight glints suddenly off something metal and blue leaning against the back porch.

It's Alex's dirt bike, untouched in ten weeks.

A lump forms in my throat. The pain is still so fresh. But I quickly push it out of my mind—when I hear another *clank* echo from farther out on the property.

I start following the dirt path that winds along the fields, toward our old barn. Crickets bombard my ears. Mosquitoes gnaw at my face. But I keep going, rifle aimed and ready… even when I reach the old tire swing hanging from that giant oak tree. The site of that framed picture of Alex I love so much. My eyes burn….

But I hear yet another *clank*. Even louder now.

I'm getting close. But to what?

Finally I see something strange. *Light.* Coming from inside our ancient woodshed, peeking through the cracks. The shed is rotting and practically falling apart. Plus, it doesn't have a power line running to it—so where's the light coming from?

I carefully approach. The door is open just a crack. I hear the hum of a diesel generator powering what I think is a set of work lamps. I can barely make out a male figure, backlit, hunched over what looks like a bumper.

I'm so confused. A strange car? A generator? What the hell is it?

I ready my rifle—when I accidentally bump the door with the muzzle.

The figure spins around. I get ready to shoot.

It's my brother.

"Stevie?" I say, throwing open the door, just as surprised as he is.

"Jesus, Molly! I almost jumped out of my skin."

I enter the shed and look around. Up on cinder blocks is what appears to be a 1990s-model Ford Taurus, a silvery blue, badly rusted one. Its hood is open, its engine in a state of chaos, tubes and wires lying everywhere.

"What the hell is all this? It's one o'clock in the morning!"

Stevie glances down at his watch. "1:15," he says a little sheepishly.

Has it only been a few minutes since I crept out of bed? It feels like closer to an hour.

Stevie looks away and starts wiping grease off his hands with an old rag. He seems embarrassed, like a little boy caught sneaking candy before dinner.

"I...I don't understand, Stevie. Whose car is this? Where did it come from? What were you...?"

I trail off when I start to piece it together.

Alex's sixteenth birthday is—well, *was*—just a few months away. He'd be getting his driver's license.

And metallic-blue was his favorite color.

That lump in my throat comes back with a vengeance.

"Buddy of mine from the refinery had it sitting on his front lawn," Stevie explains. "Few months ago, I gave him a hundred bucks for it. When Alex was at school one day, and you were off at the market or somewhere, I had it towed. Then me and Hank pushed it into the shed. I've been working on it here and there since."

Stevie pauses, then somberly runs his hand along the rusty blue siding, like a horseman saying good-bye to a beloved steed that has to be put down.

"I was gonna surprise him. Surprise both of y'all. But tonight…after we talked…I couldn't sleep, either. Figured I should finally start stripping it for parts."

I know my brother isn't much of a hugger, but I can't help myself. I wrap my arms around his giant frame and hang on as tight as I can. He embraces me back.

"He would've loved it so much," I say.

We pull apart, a little awkwardly. Stevie looks at his watch. "I should probably get some shut-eye. I can finish this up over the weekend."

But as he starts putting away his tools, I look over the car and get an idea.

"Not so fast," I say. "You really think you can get her running again?"

Stevie nods.

"'Cause you heard my plan," I continue. "First thing we're gonna need…is a getaway car."

4 MINUTES, 25 SECONDS

I'D NEVER AIMED a gun at another person before.

"This ain't a toy, Molly," my father told me the very first time he taught me to shoot, passing his old Smith & Wesson Model 10 from his rough, giant hands into my soft, tiny ones. "Unless your life's in danger, don't never point it at nobody. Hear me? Else I'll slap you so hard, your pretty eyes will pop right out of your skull."

It was a warning I never forgot.

As I hold that same S&W now, feeling the cold wooden grip in my palm, I can hear my father's words. What would he think if he knew what I was planning?

I wasn't just about to point the weapon at another person.

I was going to wave it around at *many*.

And threaten their lives.

"It worked!" Hank exclaims, a nervous grin creeping across his face.

Of course it did. I thought of the idea myself.

Hank is sitting in the driver's seat of a recently refurbished

1992 silver-blue Ford Taurus that has since been repainted black and has had its license plates removed and VIN numbers all scratched off. "They're calling in backup," he continues. "Y'all should go now if—"

"Hush," snaps Stevie, from the back.

We're all listening closely to a police scanner resting on the dash. I can't make heads or tails of all the squawking and static. Thankfully my brothers and Nick and J.D. can. And apparently, they like what they hear.

"Here comes the cavalry," says J.D.

And just like that, I hear a distant police siren. Then another. Then the glaring whine of a fire truck. The shrill alarm of an ambulance.

More voices crackle over the scanner, frantic. I manage to pick out a few words: "courthouse," "suspicious package," "evacuation," "all available units."

"Masks on," Stevie orders. "*Now* we go. And remember: in and out, *four minutes*. Just like we practiced."

The five of us don the cheap rubber Halloween masks we've been holding, each the cartoonish face of a different former president. Me, Stevie, Hank, J.D., and Nick become Lincoln, Washington, Nixon, Reagan, and Kennedy.

Hank stays behind the wheel of the parked car as the rest of us get out. I'm tingling with nerves as we cross the quiet street. And ready our weapons.

Five ex-presidents are about to rob a bank.

We burst in through the Key Bank's front entrance—and

Stevie immediately blasts a deafening round of buckshot into the ceiling.

"Hands up and keep 'em high!"

We quickly spread out and take our positions, just like we'd rehearsed multiple times in the old barn back on our farm, three big counties away.

People scream and panic—but obey.

Nick barks at the young, dumb security guard: "That means everybody!"

The kid must be barely out of high school—*just a few years older than Alex was,* I can't help but think. The way his baggy uniform hangs off his rail-thin frame, he looks like a child playing dress-up with his daddy's clothes. He flashes Nick a filthy look but meekly raises his hands.

So far, so good.

"Start emptying your drawers," Stevie orders the three tellers. J.D. tosses each of them a burlap sack.

Then my brother turns to the stunned branch manager, a sweaty middle-aged Hispanic man in a cheap tan suit and bolo tie. "*We're* gonna go open the vault."

Stevie accentuates his point with a pump of his shotgun.

"Not a problem," the manager gulps, then adds with a shaky smile, "Mr. President." He and Stevie disappear into the back office.

J.D. watches over the tellers hurriedly stuffing cash into the brown bags.

Me and Nick keep our guns on everyone else, all frozen like

statues reaching toward the sky. I realize the pimply-faced security guard's pistol is sitting in its holster....

But it's the patrons I'm worried about more. After all, this is Texas. I'd bet a few are packing concealed heat.

Last thing we need is for one of them to decide to use it.

Through the eye slits of my hot, sticky rubber Lincoln mask, I keep scanning these fifteen or so unlucky folks. The older African American married couple, the man whispering comforting words to his whimpering wife. The trashy-beautiful young white girl, maybe a cocktail waitress, maybe a stripper, still wearing her stilettos from the night before, holding the wad of one-dollar bills she was planning on depositing. The sixty-something balding fat man with the suspicious bulge under his leather jacket, and the darting eyes of a military veteran.

Any one of these people could mean trouble. (The sight of any mothers with children in the bank would be the kind of trouble I don't know if I could handle.) I keep scanning the group, looking for the tiniest hint of it. *Praying I don't see it.*

Then two more police sirens echo in the distance.

"Did one of y'all hit your panic button?!" J.D. angrily asks the tellers.

The bankers shake their heads. Yet they and the customers look hopeful as a cop car whizzes by outside...but keeps driving. J.D. smirks.

"'Course one of you did. Probably *all* of you. But it don't matter. Plainview PD's a little tied up right now."

Still, I steal a glance at my watch. Since we left the car, it's been three minutes, twenty-six seconds. In and out in *four,* tops—that was how we practiced it. Distracted across town or not, the law is going to show up eventually.

And if they do, God help us.

What in the hell is taking Stevie so long in the vault?

My breathing starts to pick up. The sweat on my brow I can't wipe away stings my eyes. This plan—*my* plan—was supposed to be foolproof....

"Let's roll!" I hear my older brother shout.

Finally.

Still holding the manager at gunpoint, Stevie emerges from the back office. A small black duffel bag, bulging with bills, is slung over his shoulder.

"Pass 'em over, come on!" J.D. commands the tellers, quickly collecting the burlap sacks.

Nick and I give the cowering patrons and jittery security guard one final look.

Then the presidential bandits head for the entrance.

Holy shit, I think. *We pulled off step one!*

Outside, the coast looks clear. Hank is just rolling up in the black Taurus.

The vehicle that was supposed to be my son's first ride...*is now our getaway car.*

I push open the bank's door.... We're so close....

When I hear behind us a trembling voice—and the chambering of a bullet.

"Don't move or, or...I'll shoot!"

15 SECONDS

I STOP IN my tracks and glance back. We all do.

Goddamnit.

That scrawny security guard had decided to play hero.

"Bad move, son," says Stevie, real low, turning slowly around.

"I said don't…don't move! I swear I…I'll shoot *all* of y'all!"

It's five against one. Not likely. But the black SIG Sauer in the guard's freckled hands is shaking so much, I'm worried he might drop it—and God knows who a stray round might hit or what might happen next.

I hate to admit it, but part of me feels almost bad for this young man. Maybe it's my maternal instincts. Maybe it's how close in age he is to Alex. I know he's standing in our way to freedom. I know he could ruin everything. But still…

"Put…put down your weapons!" he stammers.

Stevie raises his voice. "Gonna give you one more chance to let us walk."

But the guard doesn't blink. "No, see, I'm gonna give *you* one more chance—"

"We ain't got time for this shit!" J.D. snaps.

He's right. *Every second we waste…*

And Stevie knows it. So he acts fast.

In a flash, he drops to his knees and takes aim at the guard over his duffel bag.

The guard panics and shoots—clear over Stevie's head—shattering one of the glass doors behind us.

Stevie fires a single shotgun blast into the bank's wooden floor—intentionally strafing the kid's right foot.

The guard groans and hunches over. His pistol clatters to the floor.

"You just got shot for bank money," Stevie says. "Sorry about that."

Then the four of us book it like hell.

We pile into the black Taurus. I've barely shut the door before we're burning rubber.

We did it! I think, ripping off my hot, slimy Lincoln mask, adrenaline still coursing through my veins.

And all told, it was easier than I thought.

Now comes the hard part.

5 MINUTES, 5 SECONDS

"GODDAMN, THESE ARE some tricky sons of bitches."

Special Agent Mason Randolph barely nods at the ob-
servation—because he'd reached that same conclusion hours
before he even stepped foot inside the bank.

He came to it before his team boarded the Bureau-owned
Gulfstream bound for Plainview. Before he even took his
cowboy-booted feet off his desk on the third floor of the FBI's
El Paso field office.

As he told his colleagues as they sped toward the local air-
field, sirens blaring, Mason was aware they were dealing with
some smart-as-hell bank robbers the moment he heard about
the simultaneous bomb scare on the other side of the city.

But that didn't worry him. In fact, he was *looking forward*
to the challenge.

Mason had built his meteoric eighteen-year career at
the FBI by cracking the Southwest's toughest cases. Serial
killers. Kidnappings. Drug trafficking. *Human* trafficking.
Both bank robberies and potential terrorist threats—

though never a deliberately fake one, and never together in the same case.

Mason knew the region better than anybody in the Bureau. The land, the people, the culture, the criminals. And he knew how to use all that to his advantage.

He also knew just how much he'd sacrificed throughout his life to get where he was today. At forty-one, tall and handsome, with a full head of thick, wavy brown hair, he'd had plenty of girlfriends, but none of them turned into a wife.

He'd had plenty of "kids," too—*crime victims,* that is. Countless innocent people, both living and dead, toward whom he'd felt sympathetic, protective, almost fatherly.

It wasn't the same as having a family of his own. Not even close. He knew that. But solving the trickiest crimes, putting away the worst of the worst—it was worth it to him. That's just who Mason was.

Today's bank robbery/bomb threat wasn't going to be any different.

While their plane was cruising over the Texas desert, Mason and his team reviewed the facts.

Earlier that morning, a suspicious package was discovered outside the Hale County Courthouse. It turned out to be empty—except for a handful of Tannerite, a legal explosive used to make novelty exploding gun-range targets. But that was enough to get a state-police bomb-sniffing dog barking. The entire block was evacuated. Every cop, sheriff, and ranger in the county was tied up for hours.

Meanwhile, not two miles away, four armed men wearing gloves, hunting camo, and Halloween masks of four ex-presidents waltzed into a Key Bank and waltzed out with over eighty large. They disappeared into the scorching desert before the local dispatcher could find a free unit to respond.

Yep, these bad guys were smart.

"Tell me something I *don't* know," Mason replies to Texas ranger John Kim, the FBI's local case liaison, as both men step around the bank's shattered glass entrance.

Born, raised, and employed in the Lone Star State his whole life, Mason has met thousands of Texas lawmen of every stripe. But a paunchy, bedraggled Korean American one with a drawl as thick as tar was a first.

"I think that's *your* job, agent. You're the boy wonder, from what I hear."

Mason steps farther into the stiflingly hot lobby. The air-conditioning had been switched off to preserve possible evidence—which also preserves the triple-digit heat.

The agent doesn't want to spend more than two, maybe three uncomfortable minutes inside, tops.

But that's all he needs.

He scans the crime scene with squinted blue eyes. He notices two spent shotgun shells and two clusters of buckshot. Some are embedded in the ceiling tile, others near a splotch of dried blood on the marble floor.

"I'd normally suggest sending those shots to the lab," Kim says, "but why waste the taxpayers' money?"

Mason knows what the ranger's getting at. The inside of a shotgun is smoothbore. Unlike with a bullet, running ballistics on recovered buckshot or casings is almost always a total wash.

But Special Agent Mason Randolph cuts no corners, spares no expense.

"I wish I had superpowers like you, ranger," Mason says, rolling his eyes. "You can tell just from *looking*, we won't be able to pull any prints, any fibers, any DNA. Should we bother running tests on that dummy bomb by the courthouse?"

Kim sucks his teeth. Doesn't appreciate the sarcasm. Doesn't like being called out for an oversight, either.

"I heard you watched the security tapes," Kim says. "In that case, it almost wasn't worth y'all making the trip. Get anything on the suspects besides their heights and builds?"

Mason nods. "Rubber."

Kim gives the agent a funny look. "Say again?"

"Their masks," the agent explains. "It's the only lead we've got. For now."

He continues: "Witnesses say the four men had real west Texas accents. Impossible to fake to a room full of locals. Which tells me our bad guys hail from nearby. If your men want to help, tell them to start canvassing every knickknack and party-supply store for a hundred miles. Halloween's a long way off. Find me some political junkies who purchased their costumes five months early. In cash."

Kim is plenty impressed by Mason's creativity. And inge-
nuity. It's an unorthodox angle he would never even have
considered, let alone thought to pursue so aggressively. But
the ranger also can't hide his skepticism.

"Far be it from me, Agent Randolph, to question one of
the most formidable Feds in all the Southwest...."

"Then why do I feel like you're about to do just that?"

Kim forges on. "You're asking for a miracle if you think—"

"Here's what I think," Mason fires back. "We've got five
felons on the loose, who disappeared right under our noses.
Who set a trap that *all* of us stepped right into. Who, as
my colleagues at the Department of Homeland Security re-
minded me on a conference call as we drove in from the
airport, are smart enough to build a fake bomb—and Jesus
help us if they ever decide to make a real one."

Kim frowns. "Fair enough. But starting with their masks?
All I'm saying, that's haystack-and-needle territory. And you
know it."

If Mason does, his poker face doesn't betray it.

"When we find that needle, Ranger Kim—and we *will*,"
Mason responds. Five minutes in the roasting bank lobby is
far too long. "Watch you don't get pricked."

45 SECONDS

IN 1933, MY great-grandfather Joseph Rourke built the sturdy oak table that has stood in our farmhouse kitchen ever since. He probably imagined his descendants sitting around it sharing meals, stories, and laughs.

He probably *didn't* imagine them sitting around it counting out a small fortune, one that was stolen at gunpoint from a bank earlier that morning.

"Eighty-two thousand one hundred seventeen dollars!" Hanks exclaims after triple-checking his arithmetic. "Eighty-two thousand and one hundred seventeen goddamn dollars!"

A bunch of gasps and laughter fill the room. But I can't make a peep. The shock, the relief, and the thrill are overwhelming. The experience is out of this world.

"It's wild seeing all that money in one place," says J.D., in total awe.

"Crazy how *little* it looks," Nick adds, helping Hank arrange all the rubber-banded stacks of bills together into a pile no bigger than a couple of phone books.

He's right. In the movies, the bad guys' bounty is always stacked to the ceiling.

But this is real life. And incredible things seem to always come in small packages.

Then again, in the movies, the bad guys—that would be us, crazy as that is to admit—get caught in the end. There's always some tough, good-looking, plays-by-his-own-rules cop out there who'll stop at nothing to bring them to justice.

But like I said, this is real life. What we're doing is too big. Too important. It's for our home. It's for our livelihoods.

It's for my dead son.

My plan is perfect. Getting caught—that's just not going to happen to us. It can't.

Or can it?

Stevie seems to be reading my mind. He picks up the notepad Hank had been using to scribble his figures on. He brings it over to the stove, lights a burner, and drops the pages into the flickering blue flame. They transform from evidence into ash in a matter of seconds.

"When'd you last use this thing, Molly?" Stevie asks with a little smile, running his finger along the top of the oven through a film of old grease and dust.

I answer quickly and quietly. "Eighty-nine days ago."

The instinct of my brother and his friends is to chuckle—until I explain that number's significance.

"I guess I just haven't felt much like cooking since Alex died."

Which sucks the air right out of the room.

I feel a deep pain in my gut as the memory of him seeps back into me. It's still so fresh, so raw. So real.

But I also feel sorry for ruining the festive mood. For putting a damper on a celebration we all desperately need. My oldest brother picks up on that immediately.

"How's Taco Bell sound?" Stevie asks. "I'm buying. Double Decker Supremes for everybody!"

The gang gets happy and rowdy again.

"Make mine a gordita—no, a chalupa!"

"Fresco Chicken for me!"

"Gotta throw in some nachos, bud!"

"Hell *no!*" I interject, brandishing a cast-iron skillet high above my head. "You bet your asses we're having tacos tonight. But they're gonna be homemade."

My family likes this idea even more. And so do I.

I still miss my precious baby boy every second of every minute of every day.

But I've missed cooking for all the other people in my life I love, too.

So tonight, for the first time in nearly thirteen weeks, dinner on the Rourke family farm looks almost normal again.

1 MINUTE

SOME SAY MIDNIGHT is the scariest hour to be in a cemetery.

They're wrong.

The scariest time is the first light of dawn. Because there's nowhere left to hide. From your grief. *From yourself.*

I just couldn't fall asleep last night. (But what else is new?) I'm sure the buzz from the morning's bank robbery was part of it. But maybe my guilt was, too. Not guilt from committing any crime. Guilt about feeling the tiniest flicker of happiness again. Of hope. We could save the farm.

That my "hell of a plan," as Stevie once called it, might work.

I was still tossing and turning when the old clock radio beside my bed read 2:30 a.m. Normally I'd tough it out and keep lying there till dawn, when I'd finally decide to drag myself out of bed and officially start my day.

But last night felt different. I *couldn't* just keep lying there.

I had to get up now. Had to go somewhere. And I knew exactly where.

I hopped in my truck and drove the twenty-six miles to Trinity Hills Cemetery. I parked outside the front gate and walked the rest of the way in on foot.

I'd visited this place more times than I could remember. At least once every day since the funeral. Sometimes twice. On some occasions, I might stay for just a minute. Others, I might linger for hours.

I knew last night would be the latter.

As I neared Alex's resting place, my flashlight casting long, eerie shadows, the first emotion I felt was rage.

Someone left trash at my son's grave!

But as I got closer, I identified the pile of wrinkled papers strewn at the base of his headstone.

It was a stack of comic books.

Alex and his comic books. How he loved them. How his bedroom was stuffed to the gills with them, a library of illustrated stories of daring and adventure.

I figured some of his friends must have visited yesterday and left them there. That thought melted my heart.

Because Alex *adored* his friends. Even more than comics. Camping with them, shooting old bottles and cans with them, riding that blue dirt bike around with them—the one that's still leaning against our back porch. The one I still can't bring myself to move.

And his friends loved Alex right back. Sometimes, when

he'd have a few pals stay the night, I'd creep down the hall and stand outside his bedroom door. Not to eavesdrop, just to hear them laugh.

Is there any sound more perfect to a parent's ear than her child expressing joy?

These memories and so many others came flooding back to me all night long. For the past three hours, I stood, sat, paced, knelt, prayed, and cried—oh, did I cry—at the grave of my fifteen-year-old son.

But now, I start to realize the sky has changed from inky black to glowing blue. *Alex's favorite color,* I can't help but think. I hear birds begin to chirp. I look down at my cell phone. It tells me it's nearly six o'clock. In just a few minutes, this dark cemetery will be flooded with warm light.

I'm not ready for that. Not even close.

I have to get home. I have a lot more work to do.

I've only just begun.

1 MINUTE

I'VE BEEN CROUCHING and crawling with Stevie through prickly three-foot-high shrubs for the last hour. My whole body hurts like hell.

My back aches. My knees and wrists throb. Every inch of exposed skin is either drenched with sweat or scratched up by the bramble or bitten pink by mosquitoes.

But I forget all about the pain—*when I remember why I'm here.*

Step two of my plan will happen in less than a week, just a few hundred yards from where we're both hidden now: the outskirts of Golden Acres Ranch, a sprawling horse farm not far from the Texas–Oklahoma border.

Tonight, the place is teeming with some of the area's wealthiest families. Pony rides and circus performers for the kids. Grilled lobster and bubbly for the adults.

It sure is one fancy way to celebrate the Fourth of July.

And the perfect cover for me and my brother to stake the place out.

God help us if we get caught.

"I count six—no, seven—exits on walls three, four, and five," whispers Stevie, peering through the slender scope he borrowed from the top of his hunting rifle.

He's checking out the giant beige stable in the center of the property. It's not the long, slender kind I'm used to seeing. With elegant stone columns and pristine white gables, it looks more like a massive open-air mansion.

A whole lot of money passes through Golden Acres. More than goes through most *banks* in this part of the state—especially at auction time.

And we'll be coming for every penny.

"Can you make out the other walls?" I ask, still scribbling Stevie's observations in a tiny notepad, struggling to see my chicken scratch in the pitch dark.

Stevie glances at his watch. "I will any second now…"

Before I can ask what he means—*boom!*—an explosion shatters the quiet night. My heart jumps into my throat. Then a second. *Boooom!* A third. And then…

Fireworks light up the evening sky.

They light up the rest of the stable, too.

As the crowd oohs and ahs, Stevie rattles off more details about the barn. Like the positions of more exits. Their lines of sight. The locations of security cameras. The positions of plainclothes security *guards*.

I write down every word. What we've got in store for this place will make the Key Bank heist look like a cakewalk. We can't be too careful or too prepared.

"All right, that does it," Stevie says. "Let's use the noise for cover and split."

Fine by me. We slowly turn around in the brush and begin inching back the way we came, toward the road. We've barely made it a couple of yards....

"Over there!"

I hear a young man's voice. Then footsteps. Coming up on us fast.

Shit. Stevie gives me a look: *Stay still, stay calm....*

My breath catches in my chest. I crouch down even lower in the spiky shrubs. I slowly crane my head to see who's spotted us. Golden Acres security? Police?

Then I hear a girl's *giggling.* And I relax.

It's just two teenagers, sneaking off to fool around.

They collapse onto a hilly patch of grass nearby, kissing and groping, clueless that two fledgling criminals are so dangerously close.

As my brother and I scamper away, I can't help but think: *Next time, we won't be so lucky.*

1 MINUTE

AS A FORMER Miss Scurry County for three years in a row, I know a few things about putting on makeup. I've been dolling myself up going on three decades.

But this is the first time I've applied it on someone else.

"Quit twitching," I say, dabbing a glob of brown cream and smearing it all around. "You made it through Parris Island, you can deal with a little foundation."

That's right. I'm putting ladies' makeup on my retired-Marine big brother.

The rest of the room chuckles—Hank, Nick, J.D., and my sisters-in-law, Kim and Debbie. The mood is tense, and I figured we could use a little laugh.

"Don't pretend you've never tried to look pretty before, Sergeant," J.D. cracks.

More laughter. Except from Stevie. "Very funny…*Corporal.*"

I pick up an eyebrow pencil. "How about giving me a big *fake* smile, at least?"

My brother flashes a toothy grin, scrunching his face up

tight. Hank, Nick, and J.D. are all doing the same while Debbie and Kim apply *their* makeup.

I rub my dark-brown pencil up and down Stevie's laugh lines, his forehead wrinkles, his crow's feet—accentuating every nook and cranny as naturally as possible. I add a few liver spots for good measure.

I'm not trying to make my brother look good.

I'm trying to make him look twenty-five years older.

We're gearing up for our hit on Golden Acres. But this time, we won't be going in wearing president masks. Just the mugs we were born with.

Completely unarmed, too.

"Good Lord," Debbie says with a laugh. "Is this what I have to look forward to?"

She's finishing Hank's makeup. Her husband actually shaved the top of his head, to make it look like he was balding, and topped it off with a pair of fake Coke-bottle glasses. She holds her compact mirror out so Hank can see for himself.

"Damn…I look just like Pa," he says, blinking in disbelief.

Our father died of a heart attack a few years back at the age of sixty-seven. Hank's not even forty. But in this disguise, the resemblance is spooky.

"No wonder Ma always loved you the least," I joke.

More laughs all around. Then Stevie grabs my hand.

"Come on, Molly. Focus. Clock's ticking."

He's right. I finish darkening his skin and highlighting his wrinkles, making sure all the makeup looks natural and even.

Next comes the wig. Over Stevie's military-style buzz cut I set an unruly tangle of thinning gray hair.

The transformation is complete. And unbelievable.

"Well?" he asks.

"Big improvement," I say. "Never looked this good in your entire life."

Stevie checks his watch, then turns to the two women and three other "old men" standing around our kitchen.

"Debbie, Kim, every brush and pencil you used, burn 'em in the fire pit out back. Nick, you go reinspect the truck. Hank, look over the map and driving routes. Molly, soon as you're finished, join me and J.D. to review the floor plan."

Everyone has a task. Everyone springs into action. Including me.

I still have one last person's makeup to do.

Mine.

7 MINUTES, 15 SECONDS

WE'RE IN RURAL northwest Texas. But squint and you'd swear it was Beverly Hills.

A stream of Beamers, Benzes, and Caddies are pulling up to the main entrance of Golden Acres Ranch. Young parking valets politely open the doors. Out step wealthy ranchers, snooty equestrians, and fat-cat racetrack owners, all dressed to the nines.

Meanwhile, us five "senior citizens" are squished inside the cabin of a red, rusted-out '96 F-150. (It was bought on the whole other side of the state in cash, without a title, then fixed up by my brothers in the woodshed behind our farmhouse, just like Stevie had done for our first getaway car, the one that should have belonged to Alex.)

"Our truck's older than some of the kids they got working here," Hank says, steering our vehicle into the valet line.

"Don't worry," I reply, readying some cash to slip to which-ever valet parks it. "Our money's not."

As we near the front gate, each of us subtly peels off the latex gloves we've been wearing (so we don't leave any prints inside the vehicle) and stuffs them into our pockets.

I can feel the valets and other guests giving us side-eye as our truck approaches. To them, we must look like penniless old fogies who clearly don't belong. We're an annoyance. An eyesore. But beyond that, we don't warrant a second thought.

Which is exactly the point.

"Good evening, sir," says the valet as he opens Hank's door. He's wearing a Golden Acres polo shirt and can barely suppress a grimace at having to deal with us.

I slide out after Hank. "Be a dear," I croak in my best old-lady voice, "and park it somewhere close? My arthritis. I don't care to stand too long on my feet."

Before the valet can roll his eyes, I hand him the money I'm holding. He glances down at it—and perks right up. It's a crisp fifty-dollar bill.

"Yes, ma'am!"

The five of us enter the ranch.

We slip in among the other guests and dodder across the huge lawn toward the giant beige stable where the main event will be taking place. We're almost inside....

"Madam, gentlemen, stop right there."

We're intercepted by a compact man wearing a black ten-gallon hat and chewing an unlit cigarillo. Who does *not* look very friendly. Even without the two meatheads by his side—or the Colt Desert Eagle strapped to his hip—I'd know exactly who he was. (Me and Stevie had done buckets of research on this place, after all.)

It's Billy Reeves, Golden Acres' cocky, cantankerous head of security.

"Y'all don't mind if we take a few…*precautions?* This is a weapons-free facility."

Yeah, right. I know that's a bald lie. Just an excuse to frisk us, hoping to find a reason to kick us out.

But before any of us can even answer, Billy flicks his chin, and his goons start searching us for hidden weapons—patting us down *and* waving metal-detecting wands over each of us for good measure.

But none of us is packing. So they aren't going to find anything.

"Is there a problem, young man?" Hank asks, making his voice soft and scratchy.

"I'm afraid y'all might be in the wrong place. This ain't bingo night." Billy and his boys snicker. The five of us don't react. "It's a private auction. With a required reserve of seventy-five thousand dollars, in bonds or currency."

"My, my!" I exclaim now, acting surprised. "I'm afraid my mind must be going."

I unsnap the leather briefcase I've been carrying.

"I could've sworn it was *seventy-six.*"

It's bursting at the seams with stacks of cash.

Billy's eyes bug out of his head. He grunts and stammers,

pissed at being shown up, especially by an old woman. He and his men march away without another word.

All of us exchange relieved glances.

"Young people today," Hank says, shaking his head, the heavy (fake) wrinkles around the corners of his mouth creasing into a tiny smirk. "No respect for their elders."

The rest of us chuckle, happy for this brief moment of comic relief. *We need it.*

Then we finally enter the stable.

As we make our way through, I catch Stevie glancing around at all the other well-heeled auction-goers. For the first time I can ever remember, he looks a little nervous.

I quickly realize why.

Even to the naked eye, it seems like practically every person here has a suspicious concealed bulge under their jacket or vest—except for us.

So much for a "weapons-free facility."

"Looks like we really are the only folks not carrying," he whispers to me. "You still think we can pull this off?"

I squeeze his muscular arm reassuringly.

You bet I do.

3 MINUTES, 40 SECONDS

STEVIE, HANK, J.D., Nick, and I wander around the massive open-air stable.

We try to look like we're blending in with the crowd, browsing the few dozen exotic horses in their pens before the main auction kicks off.

Of course, we're actually getting a firsthand lay of the place. Reviewing the exits. Rechecking our escape route.

And looking for the one final component we still need.

We'll use the first one that any of us finds, but officially this part is my job. And I don't want to let the others down. I stroll casually through the stable but keep my eyes open wide. I peer into every stall. I look around every corner. But still nothing.

As I continue my search, I hear a horse stomping and braying in a nearby pen. I know I don't really have the time, but something about the sound just calls to me.

Part of me still has a sixth sense for animals in distress, an instinct I picked up as a teenager when I used to ride. A friend of my father's, named Angus, owned a few horses on a farm a couple of miles away. He'd let me exercise them, as long as I cleaned and fed them and swept the stable.

I had dreams of being a show jumper myself someday, maybe even owning a horse ranch of my own, so it was more than a fair deal. I loved those animals more than anything. I came to think of them as my own.

Then one day, poor old Angus had a stroke. His son drove up from Dallas, stuck him in a home, sold the farm and the steeds along with it, and that was that.

It was one of the saddest days of my entire childhood. I remember thinking, even at that young age, it was crazy and scary how sudden a life can change—mine and Angus's both. Not to mention the horses'. And how quick a person's lifelong home can disappear.

I have to remind myself: *preventing* that from happening to *ours* is why we're doing all this in the first place.

I head over to the pen. Through the bars I see a stunning brown stallion with a flowing black mane and snow-white hind legs. He's a real beauty.

"Easy, boy," I whisper. "You're not the only one feeling butterflies tonight."

I stare into the horse's big wet eyes, willing it to relax. Trying to make a real connection. I hold out my hand as an offering. Slowly he saunters over, sniffs, and nuzzles my palm.

"Now who do you think you're fooling, young lady?"

My whole body tenses. *Damn it, I'm caught, my disguise didn't work! Abort!*

"You're no horse buyer. You're a regular horse *whisperer*."

I spin, and see an elderly man—a real one—smiling at me with a set of pearl-white veneers. From his tailored three-piece suit, shiny snakeskin boots, and even shinier gold Rolex watch, I can tell right away he's got money. But his demeanor is friendly. Gentlemanly. Almost bashful.

"And such a *lovely* one, too," he adds, with the tip of his felt cowboy hat.

I realize this old-timer isn't trying to blow my cover. Far from it.

He's trying to hit on me.

"You're very kind, sir," I say, forcing an innocent smile.

"My name's Wyland. Cole Wyland." He gestures at the stallion. "Always been partial to Belgian warmbloods too. Gorgeous creatures, ain't they?"

I'm confused.

Because he's dead wrong. That's not the breed of this horse at all. Is he joking? Or just flat-out clueless? Or maybe…he can't be a plainclothes Golden Acres security guard *testing* me, can he?

"Actually, Mr. Wyland—"

"Cole, please."

"This horse here is a Holsteiner, Cole. See the *H* branded on his back leg? But mixing up the two breeds, that's a common mistake."

Cole says nothing for a moment. Should I start to worry? Did I offend him? Does he sense something's amiss?

But then he smiles even wider.

"Turns out you've got beauty *and* brains!"

All right, I think, relieved. *Enough.* I need to wrap this chitchat up quick.

"It's been a pleasure, sir. *Cole.* But if you'll excuse me…"

And I hurry off before he has a chance to stop me. I have places to be. I have a wheelbarrow to find.

I have a heist to pull off.

1 MINUTE

"ONE MINUTE TO opening gavel!" a voice declares over the P.A. "One minute!"

The stable's main atrium is brimming with anticipation. The crowd is finding their seats. The horses are getting their final primps. The auctioneer is warming up his vocal cords.

Stevie, Nick, and I hover in the wings, ready to spring into action. Meanwhile, Hank and J.D. scurry up a hidden back staircase, into the hayloft. Like most haylofts in modern stables, this one isn't functional. It's mostly for decoration.

Or in our case, *storage*.

As the audience settles in, I scan all of their faces, trying to read each one of them like I did inside the bank. Wondering who might give us trouble. Praying that none of them—like that foolish kid security guard—decides he wants to be a hero.

But with five times the number of folks—and so many clearly carrying weapons—I know the odds aren't in our favor.

The auctioneer approaches the stage, smiling and shaking hands with some of the ranch's owners and bigwigs. He turns on his microphone, tapping it a few times to test the sound.

What the hell is taking Hank and J.D. so long? I wonder, starting to fret. *Did somebody screw up? Is it not there?*

Stevie, Nick, and I trade nervous glances. All worrying about the same thing.

But then, my brother and my might-as-well-be-my-brother reappear—carrying a leather bag the size of a violin case. They rejoin us. They unzip it.

Inside is a cache of high-tech assault rifles fit for a team of Navy SEALs.

I've been around guns my whole life—but I've never seen any like this. Compact and boxy, fully collapsible, and made of lightweight green titanium alloy.

We all put our latex gloves back on as Hank hands the weapons around. J.D. passes out the ammunition: clear-plastic magazines, small-caliber, but hollow point and deadly. We ready our rifles and flip on their red-laser sights. They were designed to increase shooting accuracy.

But we mostly want them for the intimidation factor.

"Ladies and gentlemen!" the honey-voiced auctioneer says into the microphone. The crowd whoops and applauds. "Welcome to Golden Acres!"

That's our cue.

4 MINUTES, 35 SECONDS

"NOW PLEASE WELCOME our first animal of the evening. Sebastian, a playful two-year-old Kiger Mustang from—"

Stevie strafes the atrium ceiling with automatic gunfire as we storm the place.

"Hands up and keep 'em high!"

Fear and panic fill the stable. People shriek and gasp and crouch and cry. Some try to flee. But within seconds we've all gotten into position, guarding every exit.

"No one move an inch!" Stevie bellows, stepping onto the stage, assuming the role of master of criminal ceremonies.

"Anyone even *tries* to draw, we'll take you out!"

The rest of us train our weapons on the anxious crowd… on the auctioneer…on furious Billy Reeves and his bumbling security team—our scopes' thin red beams slicing through the dusty stable air like a scary laser-light show.

"Now, this can be short and painless…or the opposite," Stevie continues. "Every one of y'all here with cash or bearer bonds, start passing them down to the aisles. My colleagues will be coming through to make a little collection. Try anything funny…anything at all…"

Stevie fires off another flurry of bullets into the rafters.

More screams of terror echo all around us.

But the audience begins following his orders. Briefcases, purses, and bank ledgers are all slowly handed down.

"Let's go!" Stevie barks. "Pick it up, pick it up!"

J.D. and I move up and down the aisles, making multiple trips, each time collecting as much as we can carry with one arm—our other hand aiming our rifles. We dump all the wallets and handbags at the feet of Hank and Nick, who start emptying each bag into a giant wooden wheelbarrow that I'd found out back behind the stable.

On one of my trips, I make eye contact with Cole Wyland, the friendly old man who tried flirting with me back by the horse pens.

He gives me a filthy look. I just shrug.

Sorry, Cole, I think. *Guess you got unlucky twice today.*

Up and down the aisles we go. I'm getting a little winded. My arm's getting a little tired.

I check my watch: we've been doing this for almost four full minutes.

We're still keeping a sharp eye on the audience—especially Stevie, from his elevated perch on stage—but with all the moving around we've been doing, it's possible one of them has secretly pulled out a cell phone to call the law.

Or maybe they pulled out a gun—to try to take the law into their own hands.

Stevie seems to have the same thought. "All right, let's giddyup now!"

J.D. and I drop whatever remaining bags we're holding, and us five "old fogies" assemble by the wheelbarrow, which is now practically overflowing with a small mountain of money.

We take triangular formation around it, just like we practiced—and just like Stevie learned in the Marines when escorting a VIP: Nick pushing, Hank in front, me, J.D., and Stevie walking backward in a crescent shape behind it.

"Folks, enjoy the rest of your night," Stevie calls out as we move toward the exit. We're almost through the doorway....

"No chance in hell y'all get away with this!"

My eyes dart to the source of that raspy, familiar voice.

A furious Billy Reeves is taking a step in our direction, his hand hovering over his holstered Desert Eagle.

"Billy, don't even think about it," Stevie warns, aiming the red beam of his assault rifle directly in the center of Billy's glistening forehead. Billy gulps.

"We're gonna hunt y'all down! *I'm* gonna hunt y'all down for this!"

But we ignore his threats and keep moving. His ragged voice rings out again—*"No chance y'all get away with this bullshit!"*—as we make it outside into the warm night air.

We pick up the pace now, almost jogging across the property, leaving a trail of fluttering cash in our wake.

The bored valets, sitting around, chatting, messing with their smartphones, are beyond shocked to see us—and our guns.

Hank points his rifle at them, just in case—"Don't try nothing!" he barks—as we race over to our pickup truck, parked in a prime nearby spot thanks to my generous tip.

As Stevie, Nick, and J.D. hoist the wheelbarrow up into the cargo bed, I leap in and cover it with the heavy tarp we'd rolled and stashed back there, trapping our new fortune underneath it.

Hank slides behind the wheel and with a spare key he's been carrying starts the growling engine.

"Look!" J.D. shouts, pointing back the way we came.

Billy, some security guards, and a few brave auction attendees have exited the stable and are charging toward us, shouting and cursing, waving their handguns in the air like in an old Western, itching for a shoot-out.

They're a good ways away. A hundred yards or so at least. None of us are too worried about their aim....

But then one of them pulls the trigger.

Ping! A bullet ricochets wildly off the metal siding of our truck, right next to where I'm sitting—and I yelp and duck down out of instinct.

Christ, that was close!

Hank has put the truck into gear. We're about to drive off to freedom—but the sight of his baby sister getting shot at sparks a rage in Stevie I've never seen.

With a furious grunt, he takes aim and lays down a deafening carpet of automatic gunfire across the grass—just inches in front of Billy and his clumsy posse's paths—sending them screaming and stumbling and scrambling for cover.

Damn, do I love my brother sometimes.

"Let's roll!" he yells to Hank, and the truck peels out.

4 MINUTES, 10 SECONDS

WE'RE SPEEDING DOWN the interstate...in a white Dodge Caravan.

Nick stashed our second getaway car earlier this morning behind a rest stop at the three-way junction where State Highways 60, 33, and 83 all meet. Hank parked our red pickup to make it look like we were heading north, when really we went west. The cops will figure that out eventually, but it might slow them down at least a little.

And given the amount of money we just lifted, we'll take every single second we can get.

All of us are still buzzing after another flawless heist.

"Shit, we really did it!" Hank exclaims, drumming the steering wheel with excitement. "How much do you think we got?"

We'd removed the minivan's back row of seats last night so we could easily slide in the wheelbarrow. Nick, J.D., and I are back there now, on our knees, rubber-banding the heaping mound of cash and bearer bonds into neat stacks and stuffing them into duffel bags.

"Half a mil, easy," says Nick.

"Try *one* and a half mil," says J.D.

I don't say anything. I'm astonished by both of their estimates.

But I push that amazement from my head. Right now, we've got to stay focused on the task at hand: getting our booty bundled before we reach our next getaway car—which is "about ninety seconds out!" Stevie informs us.

I try to work faster. But I do ask: "What are the cops saying?"

A police scanner is resting on the dash, just like during our bank robbery. But I still haven't learned to decipher all its static and garbled chatter.

Stevie's sitting shotgun, keeping an eye on the road and an ear on the transmission. "They're looking for us, all right. But in all the wrong places. For now."

Ninety seconds later, right on schedule, Hank slows the van as we near our third and final vehicle, a silver '99 Chevy Impala parked just off the highway shoulder.

We all leap out, toss six overstuffed duffel bags into the trunk, then pile in ourselves.

We're soon cruising down an empty back road, speeding past miles and endless miles of Texas farmland in every direction. Once we hit State Highway 70, it will be less than four hours till we're back in Scurry County.

Less than four hours till we're home.

My adrenaline rush is finally starting to fade. I yank off my itchy gray wig and close my eyes.

I can make out every bump and crack in the asphalt. I can hear every tick and purr of the engine. I start to feel calm. Almost peaceful.

Until an image of Alex pops into my head.

For a split second—maybe it's because I have my messy wig in my lap—I glimpse *his* unruly mop of brown curls. His peach-fuzzy cheeks. His megawatt smile—which I'd give away every penny we just got to see again, for just one second.

A single tear runs down my cheek. I wipe it away, smearing my old-lady makeup, remembering why I *really* started doing all this in the first place.

The biggest and hardest part of my plan is complete.

Now we'll just have to see if it worked.

5 MINUTES, 30 SECONDS

SPECIAL AGENT MASON Randolph had just stepped in one heaping pile of shit.

No, not the actual kind. He'd spent enough time on farms and ranches in his forty-one years to know never to take a single step without looking down.

But it had been over two months since the Key Bank stickup in Plainview, and he and his team were still at square one.

Until now.

With no real leads, but no repeat robberies, either, many in his department had started hoping it was a one-off thing. A single crime committed by a couple of ballsy amateurs who just happened to get real lucky.

But as Mason had argued in staff meeting after staff meeting, he never bought that for a second. He firmly believed the Bureau was chasing some exceptionally smart and special bad guys...*who were only getting started.*

He begged and pleaded to keep the case active, and to put more bodies on it. But around week six, his supervisor pulled the plug.

So Mason kept working the investigation *on his own time*. Coming in early and staying late to follow up leads all by himself. Calling in every favor he had to interview more witnesses and canvass party-supply stores to find who bought those masks.

The fact was, when Mason Randolph sunk his teeth into a juicy case like this one, he was like a pit bull with a raw steak: he was *never* going to let go.

Until justice was served.

He was convinced the suspects were going to strike again. The moment he heard about Golden Acres, he knew they had.

With a sense of déjà vu on the Gulfstream plane ride to the nearest airstrip, Mason explained to his team his rationale for linking the two cases. Similar M.O. Similar five-person squad. Similar language ("Hands up and keep 'em high!") said with a similar west Texas twang.

The bank and horse ranch were hundreds of miles apart. But with a new crime scene and new witnesses, there was hope the case might finally take a real step forward. They just might catch these guys—*and* recover the $1.2 million that had literally been wheeled away.

Mason, his colleagues, and the entire Bureau let these sons of bitches slip away once already. He was *not* going to let that happen a second time.

No matter what it took.

"Good to see you again, Mr. Reeves," Mason says, flashing a cheeky smile as he approaches the ranch's crusty, cigarillo-chomping security head. "Feels like it was just last week."

Billy is being fingerprinted by an FBI tech at a mobile crime-scene lab in order to exclude his prints from the investigation. He growls, angry and humiliated.

In fact, Mason *had* seen him just last week. Near this very spot, too.

The agent had been in Amarillo on an unrelated homicide when a colleague in Narcotics passed along a tip. Rumor was, the Golden Acres' annual private horse auction was going to be hit. Hard.

Mason disliked crime of any sort—especially the preventable kind. So he made the seventy-minute drive to the ranch personally, off duty, for a little sit-down with Billy.

But the grizzled, arrogant bastard couldn't care less. Billy assured the agent that his team was the best in the business. And besides, even if somebody *did* try to pull something during the auction, most of the crowd would probably be packing more firepower than they were.

Lotta good that did.

"What do you want, Agent Randolph?" Billy snarls. "I already gave my statement three times. I screwed up. All right? You happy? How much I gotta say it? Y'all get off on hearing me talk shit about myself, is that it?"

"Actually, sir," Mason says, calmingly, "I came to offer you an apology."

Billy frowns. Cocks his head. Definitely not what he expected to hear.

"When we met last week," Mason continues, "I failed to impress upon you the urgency of the threat to your auction. I'm sorry. If I had, I'm sure you and your boys would've increased the ranch's security and prepared for it accordingly. Probably would've thwarted it, too."

Billy eyes Mason. Warily, then appreciatively. "Damn right we would've. Thank you, agent. You're a good man."

And you're a stupid one to believe me, Mason thinks. Billy didn't listen to a damn word he'd said. Practically laughed in his face. If anything, this two-bit gun-toting cowboy owes *him* an apology.

But Mason keeps those thoughts to himself. He knows there's no point in going to war with one of the best witnesses he's got. So today, *he'll* be the mature one. Besides, a big reason he got to be one of the region's top agents in the first place is his finely honed instinct for when to use vinegar and when to use honey.

"If you think of anything else, Mr. Reeves, you've got my card, right?"

With a tug on the brim of his cowboy hat, Mason heads out the door.

Next, he walks all around the ranch's grounds, silently taking everything in. He works best this way: soaking in the big picture, gradually narrowing in on the little stuff, and letting his brilliant mind wander and play and make connections.

Mason sees a team of white-suited techs exiting the stable holding in their gloved hands an old leather bag that resembles a violin case. Interesting.

Inside the building and across the lawn, techs are extracting bullets, collecting spent shell casings, and snapping pictures.

At the valet stand, still others are making a plaster mold of the tire tracks of what witnesses say was a mid-1990s F-150 the bad guys used to make their escape.

Mason surveys the complex crime scene solemnly.

Yep, this is one big old pile of shit. And he's up to his knees in it.

Sweating like a pig in the July Texas heat, Mason dabs at his brow with a lacy handkerchief embroidered with his initials that he keeps tucked in his suit's left breast pocket. It's old and ratty, worn thin from years of use and washing. Mason knows it's not the most attractive, or manly, accessory. He should probably spring for a new one.

But the handkerchief was a long-ago gift from someone very dear to him. And in his line of work—hell, in his entire *life*—he doesn't have all that many people who fit that description. So it's not going anywhere.

Suddenly, Mason's cell phone rings, interrupting the quiet. He answers. He listens.

He can barely contain his excitement.

"Thank you, Detective. Sounds like this case just broke wide open."

Mason hangs up and jogs back to his car.

He just might catch these bastards after all.

4 MINUTES, 45 SECONDS

I'M PARALYZED. FROZEN SOLID.

My spine has been severed clean in two.

My brain is screaming at my muscles to move, but they just won't listen.

At least, that's how it feels.

I'm standing in the farmhouse in the second-floor hallway…right outside Alex's bedroom door. It's shut. Which is how it's been for almost five months now.

I'm finally going to open it. Start cleaning out his room.

At least, that's my intention.

By all "official" measures, my son has been 100 percent erased from existence for some time now. Every last piece of paperwork has been signed and stamped and filed. His health-insurance policy has been canceled. His name as a beneficiary in my will has been removed. His meager savings account has been closed. His high-school enrollment has been withdrawn. His cell phone plan has been terminated. His

Texas State death certificate has been issued. His obituary has been published.

In the eyes of the law, Alexander J. Rourke no longer exists.

But in the eyes of his mother, he's more present than ever.

I know that feeling will never go away. And I don't *want* it to. Alex is and always will be an enormous part of my life—maybe more so now than when he was alive. His memory has pushed me to do things recently I never thought I could.

Still, his bedroom's a damn mess. (I can remember, sadly, scolding him for five minutes at breakfast the morning before he died.) It's time to get started.

I take a deep breath. *I'm ready.*

I inch my hand toward the doorknob…closer, closer… then instantly recoil when I touch the chilly brass, as if it were a hot stove.

Come on, Molly. You can do this.

I force myself to calm down. The horse-auction heist was only yesterday and I'm still pretty jittery.

So maybe I'm *not* ready. Maybe I'm rushing this, trying to do too many big things at once. Maybe if the universe sent me some kind of sign…

No. Stop it.

Okay. I try again. I rest my hand on the doorknob…

And actually twist it a half turn! The latch sticks a bit, then releases. I'm about to push open the door—

Boom-boom-boom!

I gasp, startled. Someone's on the porch, pounding on the front door.

"Sheriff's Department! Open up!"

Shit! The police! Here? Now? But how? My plan was perfect!

I quickly hurry down the steps as the knocking continues.

"All right, I'm coming!" I call, as casually as I can.

I pass the picture window in the living room and see parked in my driveway a hulking Crown Victoria, emblazoned with SCURRY COUNTY SHERIFF'S DEPARTMENT.

My heart sinks. *No…it can't be all over. Please. Not yet.*

I pause at the front door and take a moment to compose myself—and think the situation through.

If this were a raid—on the home of a suspect "considered to be heavily armed and incredibly dangerous," as we heard ourselves described yesterday on the police scanner—there'd be a whole lot more than one unit out front. The cops wouldn't knock, either. They'd bust down my door, guns blazing. So maybe they just want to ask me a couple of questions. Get a statement. Start poking holes in my story and alibi.

Whatever the reason for the police presence, I can't delay the inevitable any longer. I plaster my very best "innocent" smile on my face and open the door.

"Ms. Rourke? I'm Deputy Wooldridge. How are you?"

A man around my age in a tan uniform and wide-brimmed cowboy hat is standing on my front porch. Smiling. Sort of. He looks friendly, but a little uncomfortable.

I play it cool. I give away nothing.

"Fine, thank you. How can I help?"

"Sorry to bother you, ma'am. I'm here with a rather unusual request. It was approved by the county judge in the case. But it's your right to decline, of course."

I hold my breath. I have absolutely no idea what this "unusual request" could possibly be or what "case" he's talking about, either.

As the deputy begins to explain, he glances back at his Crown Vic—and I notice a second vehicle parked behind it. An old white station wagon. Which I vaguely recognize, although it takes me a few moments to place it.

Then it hits me. It belongs to the parents of Danny Collier. Alex's best friend since first grade. The one who texted me from Alex's cell phone when he had a seizure and stopped breathing at school.

The boy who convinced my son to smoke the crystal meth that killed him.

Deputy Wooldridge says that Danny and his parents have come to my house…because Danny would like to speak to me. And apologize.

"It's part of the deal, see, the family's lawyer worked out with the court," the officer says, almost ashamed. "He's a minor, so he's not looking at jail. But there are other penalties that Judge Thornton can impose. If Danny can show he's taking responsibility, showing remorse, acting like a man…"

I understand. But I'm incredibly stunned.

I'd heard rumors about Danny's court proceedings, but did

my best to keep my distance. And right now, I'd almost *rather* be getting grilled by the police about my role in the bank robbery and horse farm heist.

Anything instead of coming face-to-face with the last person to see Alex alive.

I can't really blame Danny for my son's death. And I don't. Like the deputy said, he's just a kid. They both were. Two foolish boys messing around, trying drugs. They were close friends. I'm sure Danny is as upset by what's happened as anybody.

As soon as he and his parents get out of their station wagon, I see I'm right.

He looks so thin, almost gaunt, and has deep rings under his eyes. His parents stay by the car as he shuffles up to my front door. Keeping his gaze on the ground, he mumbles "Hello, Miss Molly," then unfolds a handwritten letter, choking back nerves.

"Alex…Alex was like my brother. He was really cool and fun to hang out with. I loved sharing comic books with him. And camping together. He even lent me his dirt bike sometimes after mine got broken. Which was really nice."

Danny swallows hard, then continues.

"What happened last spring was the worst day of my life. It was so dumb. I see that now. I would give all the time in the world to go back and—"

"Stop, please," I whisper.

Danny finally looks up at me. His eyes are bloodshot and

wet. His lip is trembling. I can see his pain is real, his guilt genuine. I don't want to hear any more.

I can't.

Then I get an idea.

"Neither of us can go back and change the past," I say. "But what we can do, what we *have* to do…is keep Alex's memory alive. Wait here a minute."

I disappear into the house, then head to the back porch. I reappear at the front door a few seconds later…pushing Alex's shiny blue dirt bike. A peace offering.

"When you ride it, think of him. How good he was. How much he loved it."

Danny nods and takes the handlebars, almost in awe.

"I will, Miss Molly," he says, wiping his nose on his sleeve, suddenly looking ten years younger. "I promise. I will."

5 MINUTES, 5 SECONDS

MASON HATES THIS PART.

He's a crime solver. Not a speechmaker. Definitely not a cheerleader.

But every once in a while, he knows he's got to rally the troops. Especially when they're under his command.

"All right, listen up!"

As special agent in charge of the joint Key Bank/Golden Acres investigation, Mason is addressing a roomful of fellow Feds, Texas rangers, county sheriffs, and—given the tip from Narcotics and the possible drug connection—a liaison from the DEA.

The group's borrowed a small conference room at a local police headquarters in the nearby Texas town of Pampa. The room is actually a little too small to fit the dozen or so (mostly overweight) law enforcement officials stuffed inside of it. But it does meet one critical criterion.

It has a functioning air conditioner.

"I'm going to keep this quick, and let all of you get back

out there," Mason says, firm and encouraging. "But just to bring everyone up to speed…"

Mason begins by summarizing all the progress that's been made since yesterday's horse-ranch heist. The past twenty-four hours have been a wild whirlwind.

First, the serial number on the fifty-dollar bill given to the valet matches one of the marked bills taken during the Key Bank robbery.

"Given the million-to-one odds of that being a coincidence," Mason adds, "if any of you doubt that these two crimes are connected, may I suggest you go buy a lottery ticket."

Next, a red 1996 F-150 fitting witnesses' descriptions—and with tires that matched the tracks found at the valet stand—was discovered parked northbound along State Highway 83. Units initially focused their pursuit in that direction, but also swept west and south, in case the pickup truck's position was meant to be a misdirection—which many agreed it probably was. But the trail went cold.

"The truck's being ripped apart by Forensics as we speak. Nothing yet. My guess is, our perps were smart enough to wear gloves."

Mason then shares that the recovered bullets and casings have already been analyzed by the El Paso field-office lab.

Unlike with the shotgun shells at the bank that bore zero unique ballistic markings, this time techs were able to extract a wealth of information. The rounds were likely fired from a

CZ-805 BREN, a state-of-the-art, military-grade assault rifle. Though designed and manufactured in the Czech Republic, these weapons are used by elite police units and Special Forces teams around the world—including Mexico's *federales*.

"Mexico's cartels, too," Agent Marissa Sanchez of the DEA adds pointedly. "It's becoming their gun of choice. We're also starting to see more and more of those killing machines cross the border."

Murmurs of displeasure ripple around the room.

Then Mason drops the biggest bombshell of all.

Just hours after yesterday's heist, an anonymous call came in that helped pinpoint where the presidential Halloween masks used during the bank robbery were purchased: a Celebration Nation party-supply store just outside Midland.

"I sped down there to check it out personally," Mason says. "Turns out, the owner deletes surveillance footage taken inside his store after ninety days. We made it just under the wire, with only a few days to spare."

Mason plays some grainy, black-and-white tape for the assembled group. It shows an older man—wearing giant sunglasses and a University of Texas baseball cap over his long, stringy white hair—paying cash for five familiar rubber masks: Lincoln, Washington, Nixon, Reagan, and Kennedy.

"We've sent it to Quantico to run facial recognition," Mason adds. "And plastered it from here to Tucson to New Orleans. Now obviously—"

"Smells fishy to me, Agent Randolph."

Mason hasn't heard that voice in over two months.

But he recognizes it instantly.

It's wrinkle-faced Texas ranger John Kim, standing at the back of the room, arms folded across his potbelly. The same local official who led Mason through the bank crime scene in Plainview—and gave the agent more than a bit of attitude.

"Nine weeks of nothin', no leads, not a peep. Then *this*, all tied up with a bow, the same day as heist number two? I'm sorry, but I don't buy it."

"Ah. Ranger Kim. If I remember it right, you called my hunt for the purchaser of these masks…how did you put it? 'Haystack-and-needle territory,' I believe."

"I'm just saying—*why?* These guys walked off with one-point-two. Think of all the work, all the planning. Not five hours later, one of them decides to squeal?"

Mason had already anticipated that argument—and has a theory. Multiple theories, in fact.

"Maybe the leader got greedy. Maybe a fight broke out. Dissent among the ranks. Maybe an accomplice felt he wasn't getting a fair cut of the pot, so he picks up the phone to try to thin the herd."

Kim considers all that. And nods, despite himself. The agent makes a fair point.

But then for good measure, Mason adds: "I'll be sure to ask them. When I catch them. *All of them.*"

3 MINUTES, 15 SECONDS

DAMN, IT FEELS nice to have the top down and the wind in my hair.

True, I'm only going about five miles an hour.

And I'm not in a convertible; I'm steering our old green Deere tractor across the grassy fields of our ten-acre farm.

Still, I love it. I always have.

It reminds me of being a little girl again.

Growing up, there were always a million and one chores for my brothers and me to do on the farm. Pulling weeds, raking leaves, chopping wood, you name it. And like most kids, Stevie, Hank, and I would argue about who had to do what.

To put an end to our bickering, my father devised an ingenious system of sticks and carrots, tailored to each of his children's specific preferences. Whichever two of us finished all our weekly chores first got to do something we loved. The one who finished third got the opposite.

In the case of Stevie, the future Marine, his prize was getting to shoot old cans and bottles using one of our father's real rifles. His punishment was getting his fake BB gun taken away for a couple of days.

For Hank, the athlete, it meant getting to toss around the pigskin with our old man...or not being able to watch any Astros or Cowboys games on TV for the whole week.

In my case, the penalty was having to skip three desserts in a row. (I've always had a sweet tooth, I admit it.) But my reward was getting to sit on my daddy's lap while he drove our tractor around the farm cutting the grass. I'd giggle and squeal with joy as it rumbled along. I remember the speed, the sense of danger, but always feeling safe and protected in his arms.

Well into my teens and adulthood, I kept riding that tractor and mowing the lawn every chance I got. The day my father died, I drove it before his funeral. Then I did it again after the service, trying desperately to re-create that sense of security and comfort.

Which I guess I'm trying to do again today.

But also, I'm celebrating.

I'm going over every square inch of our precious farmland, savoring every single one. Because official word just came from the bank.

We get to keep it!

Apparently, the twelve-thousand-dollar lump-sum payment my family "miraculously" managed to "scrounge up" thanks to "pinching pennies" was just enough to get them off our backs.

We're still plenty in the hole. But at least we're finally in the process of climbing out. We still have to be careful, of course. We can't give in to temptation and pay back too much too fast—and give ourselves away.

But for now, we're doing all right. We can breathe easy.

The Rourke family farm is going to stay in the hands of the Rourke family!

I cruise around our property, enjoying it more than ever. The relief, the joy, the sense of accomplishment I feel are indescribable. I'm so lost in my revelry…

I almost don't notice the giant dust cloud rolling down the distant county road. This is no natural phenomenon.

I slow the tractor near the fence and watch it come toward me…*with mounting horror.*

It's a caravan of shiny black SUVs and Suburbans, each one with blue and red lights flashing in the windshields.

Well, goddamn. That's sure not the local sheriff.

It's got to be the Feds.

As I watch them pass by, panic rising, I question where they could be heading.

In any case, if they're speeding through our neck of the woods, it can only mean one thing.

They're onto us.

6 MINUTES, 30 SECONDS

HE WAS ONTO THEM.

After Mason hung up this morning with a colleague in the FBI's Digital Evidence Laboratory's Forensic Audio, Video, and Image Analysis Unit, based in Quantico, he couldn't help but punch the air in excitement.

Another one of his "haystack-and-needle territory" hunches, as prickly Texas ranger Kim might call it, had paid off. In spades.

While local and federal agents searched for the man with the long white hair in the UT baseball hat who was caught on tape buying the Halloween masks, Mason turned his attention to the phone call that had led to him in the first place.

It had come in through the FBI's national tip line, which—in order to encourage informants to be as forthcoming as possible—was *supposed* to be completely anonymous.

To many agents' frustration, it actually was.

The Bureau had plenty of other sneaky practices. It used

lots of maneuvers, strategies, and technologies that the public was intentionally misled about.

But when it came to the anonymous hotline, the protocol was airtight. Calls were recorded but could never be traced back to a specific number or location. The phone system was deliberately stripped of that capability altogether, just in case any overzealous agent ever got the idea to try.

Which was fine by Mason. He understood the reason for the policy and respected it. He was always a play-by-the-rules kind of agent anyway. To do otherwise, he felt, was sloppy and reckless. Mason was clever. Creative. Incredibly thorough. He was meticulous. At times he could be almost obsessive.

But he always followed proper procedure. *Always*. That's how his career rose so high so fast. And as important as this case was, it wasn't going to be any different.

So Mason couldn't *trace* the anonymous call.

That didn't mean he couldn't *listen* to it—very, very closely.

Three big clues jumped out right away. The male caller spoke in a whisper but had the same distinct west Texas accent as the robbers. Second, an approaching train whistle could be heard in the background. Third, the call ended with the unmistakable *chunk* of a plastic handset being hung up in a metal cradle.

Which was excellent news. It meant the call was likely made from an old pay phone, not a cell. That meant it was made in public. And *that* meant possible witnesses.

Mason and his team got to work. They reached out to Amtrak and every private rail transport company in the Southwest. They carefully mapped the exact locations of every single train in west Texas on the date and time (3:19 p.m.) the call was placed.

Then, they cross-referenced the locations of all the region's working pay phones. There are so few of them left in service, this proved a lot easier than they'd thought.

Before long, they'd narrowed it down to three possible pay phones—in Garza, Dawson, and Scurry Counties. Forensics teams were dispatched. They pulled hundreds of different prints off the Garza and Dawson phones…but only about a dozen from the Scurry one, located outside a grungy Shell station, which suggested to Mason it had fairly recently been wiped clean.

He instructed an agent to place and record a similar call from that pay phone at precisely 3:19 the following day, making sure to include the approaching train whistle and hanging-up noise for digital analysis.

Just this morning, a tech from the FBI's cutting-edge audio lab back in DC phoned Mason to tell him that, with a statistical certainty of 96.3 percent, *the sounds were the same.*

That was the Mason Randolph way. Deliberate. Methodical. *Successful.*

Mason had been driving along I20 for the past three hours. An endless stretch of flat, brown desert in every direction, not unlike the surface of the moon.

But right now, he's crouching next to a bit of shrubbery

growing along the side of the highway. His vehicle is pulled over on the shoulder, its hazard lights blinking.

Something in the underbrush caught his eye, and he simply had to stop.

With a contemplative sigh, Mason places the item into a large plastic evidence bag, careful not to disturb it. He stands. He's wearing mirrored aviator sunglasses but still has to squint. The blinding midday sun is that damn bright.

Back in his SUV, the evidence bag sitting on the passenger seat next to him unsealed—two gross violations of FBI policy the agent typically reveres—Mason is nearing the end of his drive. He's on his way to Scurry County to rendezvous at the Shell station with some fellow agents already following up leads and interviewing possible eye-wits.

But when Mason turns off Exit 174, he passes a sign that reads BIG SPRING—HOWARD COUNTY…not "Scurry."

In fact, he passed the Scurry exit some eighty miles ago—and kept on going.

Mason parks his SUV in front of a well-kept double-wide mobile home, situated on a modest plot of trimmed grass. He gets out, taking the plastic evidence bag with him. He rings the doorbell. He waits.

The door is finally opened by a petite, kindly woman of seventy-two with long gray braids.

"Mason?! Is it really you?"

She stands frozen, her jaw hanging open in total surprise. "I…I don't believe it!"

"Hey, Ma."

Mason engulfs his mother in a tight embrace.

Pamela Randolph practically squeals with delight. When their hug finally ends, she takes a step back. Dabbing away happy tears, she gives her son a long look. The tailored suit. The shiny FBI badge on his belt. The dazzling smile.

"My handsome little boy…"

"You don't look half-bad yourself."

Pamela playfully swats at Mason, then turns around and calls into the trailer: "Joe, come quick, Mason's here!"

"Who?" a voice hollers back gruffly.

"Mason!"

"You tell that bastard whatever he's selling, we don't want it!"

The tiniest tense pause—then Mason and Pamela both burst into laughter.

It's an old family joke. Years ago, when Mason was barely out of the academy, he was stuck working a major white-collar case in Houston over the holidays. It didn't look like he'd be able to make it home in time for Christmas, but after driving across the state for seven hours straight, Mason arrived just as his family was sitting down to Christmas Eve dinner. Since his cell phone had died, all he could do was ring the bell and pound on the door—which his father at first refused to answer, thinking it must be carolers or donation seekers or some kind of exceptionally rude traveling salesman.

All these years later, the joke was still trotted out any time Mason showed up at his childhood home unannounced. Sure, it had gotten a little cheesy at this point. A little predictable. But Mason didn't mind at all. Consistency, dependability, steadfastness—these were qualities he loved so much in his parents, married fifty-one years.

"Don't just stand there, silly. Come in, come in!"

It breaks Mason's heart, but he has to decline.

"Wish I could. But I'm working. I just stopped by to give you these."

Mason removes the contents of the evidence bag, and Pamela's eyes light up.

It's a loose bouquet of local wildflowers, picked along the roadside: brown-eyed Susans, mountain pinks, blackfoot daisies, white asters.

As she takes them with a giant smile, Joe Randolph totters up to the doorway—slowly because of his arthritis and the oxygen tank he's got to wheel along with him, but quick as he can because his son is there.

"Gosh, it's good to see you," he says, pulling Mason into a bear hug.

"You too, Pop. How're you feeling?"

Joe shrugs. Like his son, he's not one to complain, no matter how hard life gets.

"I didn't think we'd get to see you for another two weeks," he says, changing the subject away from his health. "Lemme guess. You got a case nearby?"

Mason nods. "Chasing down a lead in Scurry. Thought I'd stop in."

"Well, we're so glad you did," Pamela says, her eyelids still fluttering with joy.

Then Joe's expression turns serious. He grips Mason's shoulder, his grasp trembling from age, but still firm as iron. He looks his son dead in the eyes.

"Whoever you're after, whatever they done…you're gonna catch 'em?"

"Pop…*you bet I am.*"

6 MINUTES, 15 SECONDS

I NEVER THOUGHT this day would come.

"Dearly beloved…"

Not in all my life.

"…we are gathered here today…"

What I mean is, I never thought this day would come *again*.

"…to celebrate the holy union of Margaret Elizabeth Rourke…"

Suddenly I feel sixteen again, as giggly as I did the first time I went to my high school prom. As beautiful as I did the first time I was crowned Miss Scurry County.

But about a million times happier than I did the first time…I was a bride.

Charlie wasn't a bad man. Just a young one. We were both still kids, foolish and drunk in love. Drunk in *lust,* really. (In Charlie's case, he was often drunk on something else, too.) When I got pregnant at twenty, he surprised me by doing what he thought was the noble thing. He proposed—even though I wasn't sure it was what I wanted.

When the county judge at our simple courthouse ceremony asked us that big final question, I thought I was being coy and cute when I said with a smile, "I *guess* I do." I understand now that was my doubt bubbling up to the surface.

I realized pretty quick that I should have listened to it.

Charlie left me and baby Alex less than a year later.

But that was a long time ago. A whole other lifetime. Today I really am marrying the man of my dreams. And I've never been more sure of anything.

He's good and warm and decent and loyal, with a brain just as big as his heart.

He supports me in every single thing I do, large and small.

He can make me laugh till I can't breathe.

But most of all, he stuck by my side and helped get me through the darkest period of my life. He led me to a light at the end of it that I never thought I'd see again.

And oh, yeah—he looks sexy as hell in his freshly pressed suit.

"*. . . let them speak now or forever hold their peace.*"

I gaze out at the people seated all around us, many of whom have trekked from far and wide to our beloved family farm, this small group of our very nearest and dearest, everyone smiling big despite the scorching August Texas sunshine.

As I scan all the faces, I become aware of just how much a true family affair this wedding is.

I'm standing under a wooden trellis built by my brother

Hank, decorated with local wildflowers picked and arranged beautifully by his wife, Debbie.

My brother Stevie walked me down the aisle—and I could have sworn I heard the manly retired Marine sniffle.

My "something old" is my own late mother's wedding veil, as light and silky as a spider's web, which we'd kept tucked in the attic all these years.

My "something new" is a lacy garter, given to me by my sister-in-law, Kim, at the tame but hugely fun bachelorette party picnic she threw for me last weekend.

My "something borrowed" is a pair of earrings lent by my future mother-in-law, a warm and caring woman I've grown so close with.

And my "something blue"…well, that one wasn't quite so easy. It's tucked into my corset. Its metal edge is pressing gently but firmly into the skin above my heart.

How fitting, I think.

It's a silvery-blue matchbox car that used to belong to Alex.

As a little boy, he played with it constantly. "Blueberry," he called it. Some children have blankets or stuffed animals they carry around for comfort. My son had a tiny toy car named after his favorite fruit.

And now *I'm* the one carrying it around for comfort. A reminder that, even in the happiest of moments, a part of me will always be in pain.

But also a reminder that, even though Alex is no longer with us in person, he is with me on this day.

He is with me *every* day.

"Who gives this woman to be married to this man?"

Stevie steps forward. "I do."

With a hug and a kiss on the cheek, and a whispered "Love ya, sis," he delivers me to my future husband.

And then comes the big finish.

"Do you, Margaret Elizabeth, take—"

"Her friends just call her Molly, Pastor," my fiancé says with a big smile. Laughs all around.

"Do you, *Molly,*" our officiant says with a warm grin.

I hear an excited rustling from the crowd behind me. The snap of photographs. This is everyone's favorite part of a wedding. Mine, too.

"...take this man to be your lawful wedded husband?"

The pastor continues—*but my body suddenly tenses with a flicker of panic.*

That one word: *lawful.*

The law. The police. That caravan of Feds that sped into town weeks ago.

My "hell of a plan" is so close to being pulled off—but the cops are closing in on us even faster than I thought!

We can't *get caught,* I think. Not now. Not ever. We've come so far. We've risked so much. To lose it all now—*no, no, no—*

"...for as long as you both shall live?"

Those familiar words snap me out of my inner panic. I try to compose myself. Those few seconds, I can tell, feel to the congregation like an eternity. *What's she thinking?* they must be wondering. *Is she having second thoughts?*

Far from it.

I want the next words I speak to be completely untarnished. All those years ago, I said them halfheartedly, with doubt and trepidation.

Not this time.

"I do," I finally say in a sweet whisper, my eyes welling with joyful tears.

"I *absolutely* do."

4 MINUTES, 30 SECONDS

"**CONSIDER EACH AND** every one of 'em heavily armed...*and willing to die.*"

In Mason's almost twenty years with the FBI, he's used that phrase to describe a group of suspects only a handful of times.

Once was a radical antigovernment militia group holed up in the punishing Belmont Mountains in western Arizona.

Another time was an Islamic terrorist cell suspected of plotting to blow up a skyscraper in downtown San Antonio.

A third was a band of ex–Mexican Special Forces operatives hired by a Sonora drug cartel to smuggle thirty-six million dollars' worth of cocaine into Corpus Christi via a decommissioned Soviet submarine. Yes, a submarine.

Now Mason was in dusty little Hobart, Texas, population just over ten thousand, applying that label to a ragtag group of bank robbers and horse-auction plunderers—not to mention suspected gunrunners, drug dealers, and money launderers.

In the past few weeks, Mason explains to his audience, the case has progressed even more rapidly. The Shell station where the anonymous phone call was placed had plenty of security cameras...but they were pointed only at the pumps and inside the convenience store—not at the pay phone out back. ("What's the damn point of even *having* them," Mason grumbled at hearing the news, "if you can't see everything?")

Still, the cashier on duty that afternoon remembered the caller well, and was able to provide a vivid description. A sketch was quickly distributed to police stations, post offices, and local newspapers all around the region. Before long, sightings began pouring in.

Right now, Mason is standing at the front of a giant rectangular room, a VFW hall located on the edge of Hobart's meager downtown. The heels of his cowboy boots click softly on the beige linoleum floor as he paces back and forth, making eye contact with each and every person seated in front of him.

The last time Mason held a multiagency briefing like this, it was in a cramped conference room in a rural police station near the Texas–Oklahoma border.

Today, *four times* that number of agents, sheriffs, rangers, and officers are gathered around and can still all barely fit.

But that's not the only difference.

This briefing isn't solely informational.

It's also tactical.

"We believe," Mason says, "the suspects are based on a farm just a few miles from here. Two or more may be blood relatives."

On the white screen behind him is projected a giant and scarily high-resolution aerial photograph of the rolling land in question: multiple acres of dirt and grass, a few scattered structures (including a small woodshed), and a short driveway leading to a modest farmhouse.

"County records say they've owned the land for decades," Mason continues. "Generations, even. And yet..."

Mason nods at Special Agent Emma Rosenberg, a nerdy, high-strung analyst on loan from the Bureau's forensic accounting and financial crimes unit—basically a CPA with a badge and gun. She simply blinks at Mason, confused, a deer in the headlights...until she realizes he wants her to speak.

"Uh, yes, right, I apologize," Rosenberg says nervously, adjusting her chunky plastic-framed glasses. "My investigation has concluded that in twelve of the past sixteen fiscal quarters, following inspection of each putative resident's aggregate fiscal assets and gross incomes, having compared them against the estate's total liability, taxable and otherwise—"

"Aw, just spit it out, Agent Poindexter!" says good old Ranger Kim with a smirk. He's leaning against a side wall, packing a wad of chewing tobacco behind his leathery bottom lip.

Agent Rosenberg bristles. She's a prim New Englander offended by this Texan's attitude. "These people," she replies curtly, a bit of a chill in her voice now, "pay far more in property taxes, upkeep, and bank fees than they earn in reported income."

"In other words," Mason says, stepping in to pick up the thread, "they're spending money they're not supposed to have. They're *criminals*. Now…"

He turns back to the projected image of the farm, using a red laser pointer to point out specific sections and features.

"As you can see from this drone surveillance photograph taken around five this morning, the compound has exactly zero unguarded points of entry. Nothing but high fences, long ranges of sight, and little cover. Entry's not gonna be easy, even if they *weren't* armed to the teeth with assault rifles."

"Nothing my boys can't handle, Chief."

That growl of a voice belongs to Agent Lee Taylor, a grizzled and unshakable former Green Beret and current commander of the FBI's El Paso SWAT team. Given the enormous risks of the upcoming farm raid, he's made the four-hundred-mile trek to plan the mission and oversee his men personally. And Mason's damn glad to have him here.

After a grateful nod to Taylor, Mason cues the final slide: an array of photographs of the multiple male suspects, each scarier-looking than the next.

"These are our targets. Memorize their faces better than your spouse's and children's. Because I do *not* want one of these ugly mugs to be the last thing any of y'all see. You're authorized to use deadly force if and as needed. Understand me?"

This elicits sober nods of understanding from nearly everyone in the room.

The agents and officers understand the orders. The risks. The stakes.

"Because, remember," Mason continues, echoing his earlier warning, "consider every last one of these sons of bitches trained, prepared, heavily armed...*and willing to die.* Which is what separates them from us. Whatever happens out there, I'm not willing to lose a single one of you. *That's an order.*"

Mason looks out at his colleagues' brave, stoic faces.

Praying it's an order his whole team can follow.

50 SECONDS

MASON WAS DYING—for a frosty glass of iced sweet tea with lemon, that is.

His constant craving for cold sugary drinks may be his one and only vice.

He's typically a man of conviction, passion, and incredible self-discipline. Yet when it's a sizzling-hot day in Texas, his mind is like an addict's: all he can think about is mainlining some sweet tea and lemon.

So after he dismissed the briefing, Mason did just that—to slake his thirst, but also to steal a few moments to gather his thoughts. After the most painstaking preparation he's ever put into a case, he knows an extremely dangerous raid is just hours away.

A few blocks from the VFW sits the Scurry Skillet, a cramped little greasy spoon that looks like it hasn't been renovated since the Eisenhower administration. Mason ducked inside and took a seat at a window booth. A stout, sassy, sixty-something waitress named Dina took his order and then raised her eyebrow.

"A whole pitcher?"

"Yes, please. Extra ice, extra sugar, extra lemon. And then," Mason added with a smile, "in about twenty minutes, directions to the men's room."

Once his thirst had been quenched, his sugar craving sated, and his waitress generously tipped, Mason stepped back outside onto Hobart's quaint little Main Street, intending to hoof it back to the VFW command center.

Agent Taylor and his team should have a preliminary assault plan sketched out by now. A second FBI drone flyover of the farm should have been completed, which will provide more detailed and recent photographs.

Word has even come in that a pair of agents in the next county over is following up on a promising new sighting of the stringy-white-haired man caught on camera purchasing those Halloween masks. But there have been so many false leads on that mystery suspect over the past few weeks, Mason isn't getting his hopes up.

Mason barely makes it halfway down the block when— *This damn summer heat,* he thinks—he starts sweating again. And experiencing a familiar beverage craving.

But there's no time. Not now. Mason has to get back.

Without slowing his pace, Mason removes his mahogany-colored felt cowboy hat, then starts to dab his moist brow with a handkerchief—that old, lacy, threadbare, feminine one embroidered with his initials, a meaningful gift from the love of his life that he always keeps tucked in his breast pocket.

Right near his heart.

The agent is about to round a corner when he hears a voice behind him.

"Mason?! How in the heck are you?"

He turns around to see a jolly woman about his age smiling big. She's wearing a floppy sun hat and oversize sunglasses, and has two small children in tow.

"Uh…I'm well. Thank you. How about yourself?"

Mason smiles back—but a little uncomfortably. This woman is familiar, her voice, her look…but he can't quite place her. Maybe the sweat dripping into his eyes makes it hard to see. Maybe it's her "disguise" of sunglasses and a hat.

Great, Mason thinks. *A Fed who can't recognize a face.*

"What brings you back to Hobart so soon?" she asks.

Mason offers a simple shrug—and a deliberately vague answer. "An FBI agent's work is never done."

As the woman chuckles, Mason tries to do some quick mental detective work to piece together who she is. She called him Mason, not Agent Randolph, so it's unlikely she's one of the dozens of local witnesses he has interviewed in recent weeks. But she had asked what he was doing *back* in Hobart….

"I suppose this town's *your new home* now."

And suddenly, it hits him. Mason knows *exactly* who this woman is.

"Yes, I suppose it is…*Kathleen*. And I couldn't be happier about that."

One of the woman's children pulls on her sleeve, mumbling indecipherably.

"Just a moment, Luke. I'm speaking with Aunt Molly's new husband."

"Aunt" isn't quite accurate. Kathleen Rourke is technically Molly's second cousin, whom Mason had only met once before and who could stay only for the ceremony.

And yes, *Molly Rourke is Mason Randolph's new wife.*

"She looked so beautiful up there. My gosh. So radiant. You both did. Especially after all y'all have been through."

Then Kathleen gestures to her adorable but nagging children. "I'm so sorry I had to duck out before the reception. Couldn't find a sitter, and these two were itching to get home."

"That's quite all right," Mason replies, mussing the younger one's hair. "It meant a lot to us that you were there. It really was a full family affair, just like Molly said."

Kathleen gives Mason a quick hug good-bye, then sets off with her brood down the street.

Which is when Mason realizes he's still holding his cowboy hat in one hand, and in the other that rather ratty woman's handkerchief—embroidered with the initials *MER,* for Mason Edgar Randolph.

He shares the monogram with his blushing bride: Molly Elizabeth Rourke.

In fact, the handkerchief was originally hers, sewn by her grandmother when she was just a girl.

Of course, Mason didn't know this when, after dating her for just a few weeks, he discovered the lacy piece of cloth tucked in a dresser drawer. He had a minor panic attack, worried his very new girlfriend might be just a little too clingy. Had she already started making him personalized accessories?

When they realized the coincidence, they couldn't believe it.

It was just the first sign of many that these two were meant to be together.

When their six-month anniversary came around, since Molly was hurting for cash so badly—there was even talk of the bank taking back her family's farm—Mason insisted they not buy gifts for each other of any sort.

Molly followed the letter of that command but ignored the spirit completely. She gave her boyfriend that "personalized" handkerchief they'd laughed about months earlier, wrapped in newspaper and tied up with string.

Mason has kept it inches from his heart ever since, a reminder of their bond and love. Even now, wearing the wedding band he's still getting used to, it's a tradition he plans to continue as long as the piece of fabric holds up.

Mason blots his forehead with it, then tucks it away. He

dons his cowboy hat. He spins and marches back toward the VFW command center.

His new, beautiful, wonderful wife is waiting for him just a few miles away.

But first, he's got to go get some bad guys.

And not get killed in the process.

3 MINUTES, 40 SECONDS

FORTY-SIX FULLY ARMED FBI SWAT agents stand counting down to combat.

In addition to an automatic assault rifle or tactical shotgun, each carries an average of thirty-two pounds of equipment: body armor, ballistic helmet, sidearm, night-vision goggles, flash grenades, zip-tie handcuffs, rounds of extra ammunition.

Yet as Mason—already sweating under the weight of the Kevlar vest hung over his torso—paces in front of this group, giving them one final mission overview and pep talk, they all stand still as statues. No rustling. No rattling. No fidgeting.

The silence is impressive. It's eerie. *It's terrifying.*

"Strike time is at twenty-two-hundred hours exactly," Mason announces. "That's less than forty minutes out. So listen up."

He commences one last run-through of the plan with his

assembled troops. He wants to explain, too, how he and the salty Agent Taylor arrived at it.

"A traditional stealth entry was out of the question," he says. "Just too damn dangerous. Too much ground to cover." He gestures to the image projected behind him of the multi-acre farm, to its endless flat fields dotted with shrubs and trees and a few run-down shacks and sheds. "Too many possible traps. We'd be far too exposed.

"So how about a full dynamic entry?" Mason asks rhetorically. "Ripping down the farmhouse doors, roping onto the suspects' roof by helicopter, guns blazing? Hell, that might very well be the start of World War III."

In the end, Mason says, he and Taylor decided on a mix of both.

The forty-six assembled agents have been divided into four groups; each will approach a separate side of the rectangular property, slowly and visibly.

Meanwhile, the farm's power is going to be cut, plunging the place into darkness.

"There are bound to be lookouts," Mason says. "So it'll be critical to observe how they react. Using your night vision and thermal imaging cameras, pay close attention to any suspect movement or defensive repositioning. If you glimpse just one bad guy running into just one shed, that's a piece of tactical intel we're otherwise sorely lacking."

But if, as expected, the suspects refuse to cooperate?

"Well, then...we'll *make* them. Four-points access, on my

order. Full sweep of the property, clearing and moving. Sniper overwatch has the green light. Tac teams are to reassemble and form up outside the farmhouse, then engage the final breach. Any questions?"

A chorus of "No, sir" echoes throughout the high-ceilinged room.

Mason takes a deep breath. Then he goes down the line, looking each of the forty-six agents directly in the eye.

"Stay smart out there. Hear me? Aim to live. *Shoot to kill.*"

And with that, he dismisses the agents. They begin a final gear and weapons check, then start climbing into the fleet of armored trucks and personnel carriers that will be shuttling them to the farm.

Mason is about to do the same…when he spots trouble.

Agent Britt Baugher, a lanky, pimply-faced twenty-six-year-old barely out of the academy, appears to be scribbling onto his forearm with a black Sharpie.

"Grading your performance ahead of time, agent?"

Baugher can only stutter, embarrassed to be caught. "I, I…I was just…"

Mason grabs the young man's arm. *B+* is written directly on the skin.

"You could tattoo your blood type on your *forehead;* it won't speed up a blood transfusion one second."

"Yes, sir, but—"

"Now I know this isn't your first time executing a warrant.

And *you* know all your medical info is on your ID badge. Or did you forget yours at home?"

Baugher looks down at his boots. "It's just…Have you heard about those ATF agents who stormed Waco? They knew the raid was gonna be rough. So they wrote their blood type on *their* arms."

"I did," Mason says, frowning. "But that was more than twenty years ago. And how'd it turn out for them? Besides," he continues, looking the agent in the eye, "none of us is gonna *need* a blood transfusion. 'Cause none of us is going to get shot. Clear?"

"Yes, sir."

The young agent nods and hurries into his assigned armored truck.

With nearly the whole team ready to move out, Mason heads over to the giant, metal-plated lead personnel carrier he'll be riding in with Agent Taylor.

But before he gets in, he slips his hand behind his Kevlar vest. He removes his flip-front wallet, which contains his FBI badge and ID card.

He slides out the roughly three-by-two-inch piece of plastic. On the front is the Bureau's famous blue-and-yellow shield. Mason's agent number. His signature. A photo of him taken a few years back, his hair a bit longer, the wrinkles at the edges of his eyes and mouth a little less noticeable.

Then Mason flips it over. On the back is printed a wealth of vital information. His age, height, and weight. His allergy to penicillin. And on the very last line, AB−. His blood type. There just in case.

"*No,*" Mason says suddenly, angrily.

Then he climbs into the armored personnel carrier beside Agent Taylor. And keys the radio.

"All units, this is Bravo Command. Let's roll out."

8 MINUTES, 10 SECONDS

THEY'LL BE HERE soon. I have to move fast.

I can't let them catch me. Not like this.

I'm curled up on the floor in a heap of tears. A few cardboard boxes are strewn around me. The emotions I'm experiencing are overwhelming—and contradictory. Relief, worry, satisfaction, dread. You name it, I'm feeling it.

I thought I was ready, finally, to sort through some of Alex's belongings.

I was wrong. *Again.*

After my failed attempt to enter his room a few weeks ago, interrupted by the local sheriff showing up at my door with Alex's friend Danny, the last person to see my son alive, I cut myself a little slack.

Then I got caught up in the wedding, and its flurry of final preparations. Scrambling to get the house spic-and-span for the few dozen guests who would soon be traipsing through it, I swept and dusted and vacuumed and polished every inch.

Well, *almost* every inch.

My dead son's bedroom was left completely untouched, the door still shut tight. And it was going to stay that way.

Until I noticed, in the wee hours *after* the wedding…

It had been opened.

This was after the last song had been played. The last drops of beer and bourbon had been drunk. The last of our friends and family had gone home. Even Stevie and Kim, who live in the farmhouse themselves, had left. (They'd be sleeping at Hank and Debbie's that night to give Mason and me the place to ourselves.)

Loopy and exhausted from all the stress and joy of that wonderful day, I didn't just let my strapping new husband carry me over the threshold. I teasingly ordered him to lug me all the way across the lawn, up the stairs, and into our bedroom. Good sport that Mason is, he happily obliged…but demanded, with a sexy wink, that I find some "creative ways" to pay him back.

We had just reached the top of the steps when I noticed the door to Alex's bedroom was slightly ajar.

I gasped. I covered my mouth in shock. I leaped out of Mason's arms, nearly tripping over the train of my wedding dress.

It was obvious enough what had probably happened. One of our guests must have been searching for the bathroom, and decided to keep the honest mistake to herself.

But none of that changed the fact that Alex's bedroom door was open.

For the first time in months.

I slammed it shut as quickly as I could, then leaned my head against the door frame. And let out a single sob.

Mason came up behind me and wrapped me in his muscular arms. He just held me as I struggled to pull myself together. It was such an emotional day already, and now this.

"Too bad we splurged on the honeymoon suite," Mason whispered with a smile.

I laughed. I had to. I needed to.

God bless this man, I thought. An average new husband might be less than thrilled at the prospect of spending what should be his steamy wedding night chastely comforting his grieving new wife instead. But Mason was anything but average. He'd managed to make a sad moment tender and loving and funny all at once.

"I'm sorry," I managed to whimper, turning around to take in his handsome face.

"Nothing to be sorry *for,*" he insisted. "That's the nice thing about spending the rest of our lives together. We'll have plenty more nights to try again."

Try again.

That's what I'm doing right now.

And failing.

Our wedding was a few weeks ago, and Mason had been gone for almost all of them, working on an important case that had taken him all over the state. But tonight was a special occasion. He was going to be nearby, he said, and had managed to get the night off. So I had decided to cook a big family dinner.

It would be the first time all of us—Stevie, Hank, Debbie, Kim, Nick, J.D., Mason, and me—gathered around the table since we'd tied the knot. It would be a celebration dinner of sorts, too. Our farm was saved. My "hell of a plan" was almost complete. Things were looking up for the Rourke family. We were all riding high.

So I decided I might finally be ready to start going through Alex's stuff.

Not his bedroom. I knew I wasn't prepared for *that* yet.

But I'd remembered my son had a few boxes of old junk hidden away in the attic, some odds and ends he hadn't touched in years. So I figured, in the hour or so it would take for the pie crust to set and the chicken to finish roasting, those boxes would be as good a place to start as any.

And so far, they seem to be. Inside I find some old textbooks and dusty paperbacks. A stack of CDs from bands I've never heard of. A tennis racquet, still almost brand-new, that Alex had used just once before losing interest in the sport forever. It's all stuff I can easily donate or throw out, without a second thought.

I'm nearly through all the boxes. It's only taken a few painless minutes.

But then I reach the bottom of the last box.

And I find something that takes my breath away.

It's a drawing Alex made when he was in first grade: two stick figures, a boy and a woman, both wearing giant space-suits, floating in the starry night sky. His teacher, Mrs. Cunningham, had written in blue marker in block letters at the bottom: "When I grow up, I want to be an astronaut, so I can go to outer space with Mommy."

Reading those words feels like a knife straight to the heart.

For so many months now, I've mourned the life that Alex had been leading in the present. I've barely thought about the one he was *going* to lead—in the future.

His dreams of being an astronaut may have been a childhood fantasy, but his future had been very real. He'd been spending time with girls. He'd started talking about college. He was going to have a career someday. A home, a wife. Children of his own. Alex *would* have reached the stars like he wanted to—in his own way, on his own terms—if only he'd had the chance.

I clutch the drawing to my chest and collapse onto the floor, letting this profound new wave of grief wash over me.

And I stay there. Paralyzed. Minutes ticking by. Tears streaming down my cheeks.

Oh, Alex. My baby. Will this pain ever go away?

I know the chicken is still cooking in the oven and my family is on their way. I know I can't lie here forever. Maybe just a little bit longer…

When I hear something outside—a vehicle pulling up in front of the farmhouse.

I look at my watch. It's early yet. The guests aren't supposed to be arriving for quite some time. Who could it be? I force myself, finally, to get up.

I walk over to the attic window and peer down. The sun is setting, and the vehicle is hard to make out. A few people exit. But I can't tell who they are.

It must be Stevie and Hank and their wives. Right?

Who else could it be?

3 MINUTES, 20 SECONDS

"THIS IS THE FBI!"

Mason is crouching behind the hood of a giant Lenco BearCat armored personnel carrier, talking into the 150-decibel speaker system mounted on its roof. He's raising his voice, but Mason could *whisper* and his words would still echo across this dark, quiet, sweltering slice of Texas for a quarter mile.

"Your property is surrounded by armed federal agents!"

That's putting it lightly.

Before beginning his callout, SWAT Agent Taylor received confirmation from all his team leaders—and passed it along to Mason—that each group had taken their positions along the four sides of the property.

"We are in possession of a search warrant for the premises and arrest warrants for all individuals on site!"

As the agents had approached, the power had also been cut to the farm—but to Mason's surprise, that didn't make much difference. The lights inside the main farmhouse went out, then flickered back on a few seconds later: diesel generators, most likely.

"This is your one and only warning! Come out peacefully, with your hands interlaced on top of your—"

"Sir, take a look at this!" whispers Agent Norris Carey, the burly thirty-nine-year-old leader of the primary tac team closest to Mason and Taylor.

He shows them an LCD screen, a live feed of a thermal camera sweeping the acres in front of them. The land is scattered with prickly bushes and stumpy trees—many of which seem to be giving off *glowing orbs of white-hot heat*.

"What in the hell am I looking at?" asks Taylor, confused and alarmed.

"I...I just don't know," Carey responds. "Trees and shrubs, they don't give off this kinda heat signature. Teams at every position are seeing the same thing."

Mason immediately knows what's happening—and snorts in displeasure.

"*Damn,* are these smart sons of bitches...."

He had witnessed this simple but effective defensive technique used just once before: on the sprawling estate of a Mexican drug lord outside Ciudad Juárez while taking part in a joint U.S.–Mexico strike-force assignment. He'd never seen it stateside.

"*Heat lamps,*" Mason explains. "Trying to thwart our thermal scopes. Gotta be wired to the generators, kicked in automatically as soon as *they* did. To hide the heat signature of any *gunmen* who might be hidden in the foliage."

"Christ almighty," Taylor says under his breath. He quickly counts up the number of heat orbs he sees on the screen. "So there could be *twelve* concealed shooters on our perimeter alone?"

"Or none at all," Mason replies. "But they know we'll have to check and clear each one. Slows us down more than coating the grass with tar."

Mason keeps his cool, but Taylor grows enraged. He grabs a subordinate's night-vision binoculars and looks out at the distant farmhouse.

"I don't see a damn one of them coming out waving a white flag," he barks.

Mason is praying tonight ends peacefully and decides it's worth a bit more breath. He keys the bullhorn radio again, and goes a bit off script.

"We all know how this is going to go down! No mystery about it. All of you on this farm are going to jail for a very long time—for what you've done, for the money you've stolen, for the people you've hurt…*for the cowards you've been!* I'm offering right now a chance for you to be *men.* Any fool can pick up a gun. It takes real *courage*…to put one down!"

Mason waits. And holds his breath, praying he got through to them. Even the gruff Taylor gives him a begrudging nod. *Well said.*

"We've got movement!" exclaims Agent Carey.

Mason looks back at the farmhouse. Sure enough, its side door has opened. A figure emerges, holding a rifle above his head…

Then quickly lowers it and opens fire.

"Damn it!" Mason shouts, ducking down behind the vehicle and reaching for his walkie-talkie.

Gunshots pierce the quiet night, ricocheting off the armored car's metal plates.

"Shots fired, shots fired!" he yells in the radio. "All units, move in!"

The giant armored truck roars to life. Mason, Taylor, Carey, and the dozen agents in their team fall in line behind it as it plows through the wood-and-barbed-wire fence along the farm's perimeter—and keeps on moving, gunfire still ringing out.

The raid is just beginning.

5 MINUTES, 15 SECONDS

A SLEEPY FARM in west Texas has become a brutal battlefield.

It's been that way for almost an hour.

Mason, his unit, and the other three teams closing in have all been slowly but surely making their way across the few acres of land toward the main farmhouse.

One bloody inch at a time.

Multiple skilled sharpshooters are perched in the second-floor windows of the farmhouse, giving them a scarily good elevated position.

The fighting is slow. Brutal. Hellish.

The Feds, even with all their training and gear and armored vehicles—and outnumbering the suspects at least three to one—are taking nothing for granted.

More than a few agents have already gotten shot and pulled out. None is wounded seriously, but the teams' numbers are beginning to thin as they get closer.

And now, they're *very* close.

The farmhouse is just a few dozen yards away.

"Two o'clock!" Mason yells, spying a crouched shooter leaning out of a prickly sage bush on their flank.

Without waiting for his teammates to react, Mason raises his M4 carbine and fires three rapid, perfectly placed shots—two to the chest, one to the head.

"Neutralized!"

The suspect is dead before he hits the dusty ground—right beside the rusty metal space heater nestled in the brush beside him.

The team keeps moving.

Mason sticks his head up and scans the terrain up ahead. Virtually all that stands between his team and their side of the farmhouse is a small, rickety woodshed.

God only knows what could be inside.

"Form up at the entryway," Agent Taylor orders, in an urgent whisper. "Two plus one. Cam it and breach, on my go."

As soon as the armored vehicle gets between it and the farmhouse, four SWAT agents peel off from the team and hurry into position: two on each side of the shack's closed wooden door.

Mason, Taylor, and the others provide cover as one of the agents slips a tiny, flexible camera—about the shape of a black licorice Twizzler—beneath the door. He rotates it all around, giving a second agent holding a smartphone-size digital monitor a 180-degree night-vision view of the inside.

"Looks clear," the agent whispers.

So Taylor gives the cue, and a third agent produces a metal

crowbar—and wrenches open the door with a wood-splitting *crunch*.

Mason watches as the four agents burst into the tiny space, the red laser beams atop their guns whipping all around, aiming at every nook and cranny.

Discarded auto repair tools and engine parts line the walls. But otherwise the shed appears empty…

Until a gunman suddenly jumps up from behind a tool chest and unleashes a torrent of gunfire.

The agents inside duck for cover and shoot back, riddling his body with bullets.

But not before one of the Feds on the outside gets hit.

"Goddamnit!" Mason groans, cupping a bloody shoulder.

"That son of a bitch get you?" asks Taylor with concern.

Mason leans his back against the rear side of the armored vehicle for support. He pulls out a flashlight and examines his wound.

His shoulder was only grazed, but it hurts like hell. Mason can feel it, the pain hot and sharp, throbbing in sync with his pulse.

"One of us can escort you back to the perimeter, sir," offers Agent Carey, the team leader. "Rest of us, we'll keep on pushing toward the—"

"Hell no," Mason roars through gritted teeth. "I wanna be there when we breach that damn farmhouse, and see the looks on those bastards' faces!"

Taylor, Carey, and the other agents are taken aback.

They've never seen the usually calm and collected Mason so enraged. So primal. It's scary.

"Jesus, Mason," says Taylor. "You're bleedin' all over the damn place. No one's been working harder to get these bastards than you have, but—"

Thankfully Mason doesn't have to argue: his and Taylor's radios crackle to life.

"Alpha and Charlie teams have reached the farmhouse," says one of the other teams' leaders. "Ready to enter."

"Roger," responds another agent over the radio. "Delta team closing in."

That's great news, and Mason and his men all know it. Two of the four SWAT units are in position outside the house, with the third nearby.

Mason turns his gaze toward the farmhouse. It's so close. *The final stand.*

"Bravo Command, copy that," Mason responds into his walkie, signaling Taylor and the others to get back into formation and keep moving. They obey.

"En route, too. Prepare to breach!"

3 MINUTES, 45 SECONDS

CLINK…CLINK, CLINK…BOOM!

The entire ramshackle farmhouse gets briefly lit up like a jack-o'-lantern as four flash grenades are thrown and detonated inside simultaneously.

"Go, go, go!"

Mason barks the command at his team and into his radio—and nearly all the remaining agents kick down doors and crash through windows and pour into the home from all sides.

"FBI!" they yell, moving in tight fluid lines from room to room like slithering snakes. "Get on the ground! FBI! Lemme see your hands!"

The *pop-pop-pop-pop* of gunshots soon rings out from inside as well, followed by exclamations like "Clear!" and "Suspect down!" and even "I'm hit!"

Mason's focus is so tightly on the farmhouse, he barely notices his wounded shoulder anymore, the black sleeve of his jumpsuit soaked in blood.

"Bravo and Charlie teams, moving upstairs!" comes a voice over the radio.

Mason and Taylor share a look.

This nightmare of a raid is almost over.

But it's not finished yet.

"We got one!" an agent exclaims over the radio. "In the attic!"

Mason holds his breath and waits. Waiting to hear those magic words...

"Charlie Leader, giving the all clear! Repeat, site is clear and secure!"

Mason pumps his fist in triumph. Taylor claps him on his good shoulder. The agents can finally breathe easy.

"Bravo Command, good copy," Mason radios back. "All clear and secure. Stand down."

And then, for good measure: "Well done, every one of you. *Damn* well done!"

Only now does Mason glance down at his bloody shoulder. But his adrenaline is pumping so hard, he barely feels it.

Slowly, the entry teams begin exiting the farmhouse from all sides. Many are carrying confiscated firearms. Others, bags and bags of crystal methamphetamine.

Finally, Mason sees the person he's been waiting for—and he's shocked.

It's one of the sole surviving suspects. In handcuffs, lip bloodied, screaming and spewing a string of profanities, being led out of the farmhouse by two agents.

"Here's the one we found in the attic, sir," says one of the escorting agents.

Mason just nods. He recognizes who it is right away.

The ringleader of the group. The criminal mastermind he'd been after all these months.

Mason can't believe his eyes. He marches right over. "Abraham J. McKinley, you have the right to remain silent."

"Goddamn murderers!" the crazy old man shouts, struggling against his restraints. "All of you! Look what you done!"

Mason ignores his theatrics and keeps going. "You're under arrest. For multiple counts of federal grand larceny, felony assault with a deadly weapon, illegal possession of a firearm, and conspiracy to commit—"

"Boy, what the hell you talking about?" McKinley demands, getting as close to Mason's face as he can. With his wild mane of white hair fluttering behind him, McKinley's resemblance to the man caught on camera buying those Halloween masks is undeniable.

"The bank robbery in Plainview," Mason answers. "The horse-auction theft. All the evidence points to you and your crew, Abe."

"Huh? We ain't never stole nothing and you know it!"

Mason just smiles. "What about distributing a Class 2 illegal drug? Word is, you and your boys have been doing that for months."

McKinley shakes his head. Then he looks back into his farmhouse, at all the carnage, inside and out. Numerous suspects lie bloody and dead. He starts to lose it. He twists and writhes in his handcuffs. The agents hold him steady.

"You...you killed 'em! You pigs killed all of 'em! Look what you did!"

"No, Abe," Mason replies calmly. "Look what *you* did."

And then, as McKinley is just about to be led away, still ranting and raving, Mason leans in close and whispers, "Because you...killed *him*."

It takes McKinley a moment to realize the bombshell Mason has just admitted.

"You...you framed me?! You son of a bitch! This whole thing is bullshit!"

Mason watches in silence, betraying nothing, as the aging meth king—the man whose gang made and sold the drugs that killed Alex—is carted away.

But then, across Mason's handsome face creeps a sly little grin of satisfaction.

45 SECONDS

THIS PART OF west Texas is as flat as a pancake. Not a hillside for a hundred miles. And most buildings in Hobart top out at two floors.

Tonight, that just wasn't going to be tall enough for me.

So I took the long drive to the giant water tower on the outskirts of town.

I parked my truck. I hopped the rusty metal fence. Then I climbed up slow and steady, all the way to the top, over eighty feet high.

Yes, I was breaking the law. But after months of robbing and shooting and evidence tampering, what was a little harmless trespassing?

I settled in and aimed a pair of high-power binoculars at a multiacre farm about a half mile to the southwest. It belonged to a band of meth dealers that, I had on very good authority, was currently being surrounded on four sides by the FBI.

Stevie, Nick, and J.D. had just arrived for my dinner party

and were helping me set the table when I got the text from Mason. It read simply: Thinking of you ☺.

When I read it, I gasped. Then rushed out the door. Alone, I insisted.

Mason often sent me sweet little text messages throughout the day, but he never, ever ended them with a smiley or winking face. He thought it was childish, not cute. So did I.

Which meant, we both agreed, using one would make the perfect secret code to alert me that the FBI's raid on the McKinley farm was a go.

For safety's sake, Mason had refused for weeks to give me any specific details about how the case against the McKinleys was developing or when the search and arrest warrants would come through. But recently he'd started dropping hints that it was close.

I always knew this day would come. I had a feeling it might be tonight, but I didn't know for certain until barely ninety minutes ago.

From my elevated perch, I watched the whole thing happen. The multiple teams of SWAT agents. The lumbering armored vehicles. The shooting. The screaming.

I prayed to God that Mason wouldn't be harmed. I prayed that none of his colleagues would be, either.

But I prayed that Abe McKinley and his boys...well, I prayed that they finally faced justice. Whatever that meant. However the man upstairs decided to mete it out.

Which was the *real* purpose of my "hell of a plan" all along.

Yes, we needed the money to pay back the bank to save our farm. Desperately.

But more than anything, *I* needed to make McKinley pay... *for killing my boy.*

And tonight, I finally did, with the help of my then-fiancé and now-husband—who walked me through the ins and outs of a federal bank robbery investigation...who planted the assault rifles at the Golden Acres horse ranch...who "discovered" the location of the pay phone Hank used to call in the anonymous tip that turned up Stevie on camera, wearing a white wig, buying the Halloween masks.

My "hell of a plan" worked like a hell of a charm.

I've been sitting on the ledge of the water tower for well over an hour. Finally the shooting seems to have stopped for good. Agents are moving in and out of the farmhouse now with ease. So are crime scene techs, and paramedics.

I even think I spy Abe McKinley himself being hauled out in cuffs, thrashing and carrying on like the madman he is.

I'd love to have seen his face when he realized what was happening. And when he realized *why*. But I'll settle for hearing about it from Mason secondhand.

I should probably get back home. The show's over, folks. I still have that dinner party to throw—and now my family *really* has something to celebrate.

I'm sure Mason is going to be tied up at the scene for hours. But he'll have to come home eventually. When he does, I'll still be up, waiting. Beyond grateful.

I put away my binoculars and stand, stretching out my cramped legs.

But before I climb down, I take out a folded piece of paper from the pocket of my jeans. I carefully open it.

It's that drawing Alex made in first grade that I just discovered tonight, of him and me floating together in outer space, the destination of his dreams.

As my eyes begin to water, all these months of pain and stress and work and agony finally coming to an end, I hold the paper to my chest.

And I look up at the night sky, a blanket of blackness dotted with a trillion points of light.

Alex, I think, *you are floating in the stars. You made it after all. May you find peace and comfort and love.*

Someday, I will be there beside you. Just like you dreamed.

But not yet.

1 MINUTE

IT'S MY VERY favorite time of the day. The world outside my window is calm. Peaceful. Quiet.

It's not quite night but not yet dawn. And I'm not quite asleep but not yet awake.

I snuggle a little more into Mason's strapping arms. He mumbles happily and hugs my body tighter.

I nuzzle his shoulder, just above the scar from the bullet wound he got well over a year ago now, during that fateful raid on the farm.

The one that resulted in the arrest of Abe McKinley and three surviving associates, who were sentenced to a combined 136 years in federal prison, at the US Penitentiary in Beaumont, Texas.

But all of that's in the past now. Ancient history. Our family farm has been paid off. The guilty have been punished. And life has carried on.

For the first time in a long while, I feel relaxed. Rested. At ease. I breathe in my husband's sweet musk. I run my finger up and down his collarbone.

I could stay like this forever, I think.

And then, I hear something. A noise coming from inside the house.

I could wake Mason to handle it. But should I?

I glance at the clock on his side of the bed—his holstered sidearm and FBI badge beside it. It's just after 5:00 a.m.

No, I decide. I'll let him sleep.

I slip out of bed and tiptoe down the hall. The sound is getting louder.

I finally reach a door that's slightly ajar: the door to Alex's old bedroom. The door I once couldn't even fathom opening.

But this morning, I drowsily push it open and enter without a second thought.

I'm used to it by now, but the space is so different from how it once was. Fresh paint, different carpet, new furniture. It's almost unrecognizable as my son's former bedroom.

Because now it's my new daughter's nursery.

Little Abby is wailing in her crib. "There, there," I coo, picking her up and bouncing her gently in my arms. "What's wrong?"

I fed her a few hours ago, so I know she can't be hungry. I check her diaper; she doesn't need to be changed. The room is a comfortable seventy-two degrees, so she can't be hot or cold. What could it be?

As Abby continues crying, I get an idea.

I open the closet, revealing stacks and stacks of comic books. *Alex's* beloved old comic books. Those, of course, I couldn't throw away in a million years.

I pick one at random and open to the first colorful page. As if by magic, Abby stops crying, captivated by the words and pictures, groping for them with her tiny hands.

"You know," I whisper, "your brother used to like these, too."

And then I begin to read.

"*The Amazing Spider-Man*. This one's called…'Brand New Day.'"

**Christy and Martin are playing a game
that's about to go too far . . .**

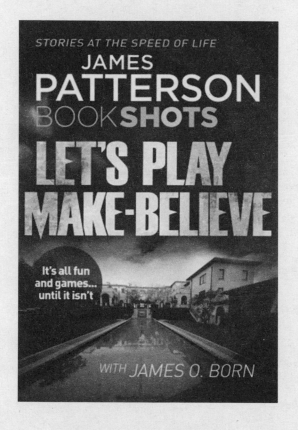

Read on for an extract

THE YOUNG REPORTER TRIED to keep her eyes on the camera as it tracked past her to the mansion facing South Ocean Boulevard and the Atlantic on the island of Palm Beach. She thought back to all her journalism and broadcast classes and tried to keep calm. Even with that effort, her voice cracked when the studio anchors cut to her live.

She said, "I am here in the town of Palm Beach as the police try to sort out what has occurred at this South Ocean residence. We know that at least one person has been shot to death, and the killer is believed to be still inside, possibly with a hostage." The young reporter threw in a few improvised lines, then hit the points the producers wanted her to make. "Police have closed this section of South Ocean, and early-morning traffic is backing up as far as the Southern Boulevard Bridge, as we wait to hear exactly what has led to the tense standoff with police on the island of Palm Beach."

Someone off-camera was directing her to step to the side so that the early-morning sun didn't reflect off the lens. As the camera panned to follow the young reporter, there was a growing crowd of neighbors gawking at the scene. Nothing like this had ever happened east of the intracoastal. Police activity of this nature was much more common in West Palm Beach or Riviera Beach. Most of the locals thought Palm Beach was immune to serious crime.

The reporter motioned for the camera to focus back on her and said, "We've heard reports that the town police chief has asked for assistance from the Palm Beach County Sheriff's Office in case they have to make a forced entry into the house."

In the background, near the front of the house, a police officer started to speak into a megaphone. The reporter stopped talking so the camera operators could pick up the audio and show the police officer crouched behind a cruiser.

"Martin Hawking, come out of the front door with your hands up and empty. No one will hurt you if you do it now." There was about a twenty-second break. Then the police officer said, "Come out right now, Mr. Hawking."

I SOMEHOW MANAGED TO slide onto a stool at one of the prime high-top tables near the front door of the Palm Beach Grill. From here you could see the bar, get waited on easily, and keep an eye out for anyone of note who wandered through the main entrance. Landing this high-top was close to a miracle on a Friday evening at seven o'clock, when the place was clogged with Palm Beachers. Julie, the sweet and personable maître d', stopped by, and I gave her a hug.

I needed a night out and a few laughs with my friend Lisa Martz. Like me, Lisa was going through a rough divorce, but she'd hit the ground running and never looked back. The whole thing had struck me a little harder, mainly because it had come out of left field. Lisa was happy to be out of her prison, whereas I'd never thought I was in one.

Lisa signaled to the waitress that we needed another round of margaritas.

I laughed and said, "That'll be my third drink tonight! I'll have to run twenty miles to burn it off tomorrow."

Lisa put her hand on my forearm and said in her sweet Alabama accent, "Don't even talk to me about losing weight. You look fabulous. When Brennan asked for a divorce, it was the best thing that ever happened to you. Everything about you has changed. You look like a cover model with those cheekbones and that smile. If you tell me you're a natural blonde, I might have to stab you with a fork right now."

I had no desire to be stabbed, so I kept my mouth shut. I appreciated my friend's attempt to build my confidence. The fact is, I had been going across the bridge and working out at CrossFit in West Palm Beach, as well as jogging on the beach a couple more days a week. My husband, who was six years older than me, had turned forty a few months ago and decided I was too old for him. He may have phrased it differently, but I'm no idiot. It stunned me then and it still stings now. But I was making every effort not to let that loser dictate the rest of my life. As my dad used to say, "Life is tough enough, don't be a dumbass."

Suddenly, Lisa was waving frantically at a guy across the room, who smiled and worked his way toward us. He was about my age and got better-looking with each step. In good shape, a little over six feet tall, he was dressed casually in a simple button-down and a pair of jeans. A nice change from the usual show-offs on Palm Beach.

Lisa said, "Christy, this is my friend Martin Hawking. Marty, this is Christy Moore. Isn't she gorgeous?"

I admit I liked the goofy, shy smile and the slight flush on Marty's face as he took my extended hand. He had a natural warmth that was intriguing. His short, sandy hair was designed for an active man: it required minimum styling. Before I knew it, we were sitting alone as Lisa got on the scent of a recently divorced gynecologist who was having a few drinks at the other end of the bar.

I said, "I'm sorry if Lisa messed up your evening by dumping you here with me while she went off on the hunt."

Marty let out a quick, easy laugh and said, "I have to be completely honest. When I saw the two of you walk in and she stepped up to the bar beside me, I asked if she would introduce us. I know her from working on the addition to her house over on the island."

"Are you a contractor?"

"No, I'm legit."

He made me laugh, even at such an old joke.

"Actually, I'm an architect. That's just a general contractor who doesn't have enough ambition to make any money. What about you? What do you do?"

I wanted to say, *Make poor choices in men;* instead I said, "I'll tell you when I grow up."

"What would you like to do until then?"

I thought about things I did as a kid growing up in New Jersey. My friends and I kept playing the same games but adapted them as we grew older. I said, "I like games." His hand casually fell across mine on the table and he looked me directly in the eye.

"What kind of games?"

I wasn't used to flirting. I felt like I was crushing it after being so out of practice. Instead of telling him about some lame game I liked as a kid, I said, "Maybe you'll get to find out."

I liked being mysterious for once, and this guy seemed nice and was enjoying it. I couldn't ask for much more right about now.

AFTER OUR MARGARITAS AT the Palm Beach Grill, we ended up at the HMF inside the Breakers Hotel. By then we were on our own, and Lisa was firmly attached to the divorced gynecologist. Marty and I just chatted over drinks. We talked about everything. It was easy, light, and fun. I even found myself opening up about my separation and the pending divorce. He told me a little about his own divorce and how his wife had moved to Vero Beach just so they wouldn't run into each other. It was a good plan.

We threw down some specialty drink at HMS that, as near as I could tell, had vodka, some sort of pink fruit juice, and a lot more vodka. Marty thought we were drinking at the same pace, but I was being much more careful.

I thought hard but just couldn't find the right words to tell Marty how much I'd like him to come back to my place. In my whole life, I'd never picked up a man for a one-night stand. It was new and a little bit scary to me, but I'd be lying if I said there wasn't an element of excitement to it as well.

He gazed at me and said, "You have the most beautiful eyes."

"That's just the alcohol talking."

"No, I mean it. All four of them are beautiful." He weaved his head back and forth like someone pretending to be wildly drunk, and it made me laugh out loud.

That was all I needed to screw up the courage to say, "How would you feel about coming back to my place for a nightcap?"

"How far is it?"

I gave him a look. "It's in Belle Glade, about an hour away."

"What?"

"No, Mr. Clueless, it's here in Palm Beach. No one's ever more than ten minutes from their house when they're on this island."

We grabbed a cab back to my temporary residence at the Brazilian Court Hotel. Although Brennan was beating me out on almost everything in the divorce based on some prenuptial agreement I signed when I really believed he loved me, he didn't want the locals to view him as a complete jerk, and he had put me up in a nice apartment inside the hotel. The cost meant nothing to him, and at least I had a base of operations on the island.

No one asked questions at the Brazilian Court, and Allie, a girl from my CrossFit class, was the evening clerk there. She gave me a heads-up whenever she saw Brennan stomping through the lobby to confront me about one thing or another and generally looked after me like women our age usually did.

Once we were in the room, I realized I was still a little tipsy. I had never used that word in my life until I moved to Palm Beach. Everyone was always getting "a little tipsy," no matter how much they'd had to drink, but in this case, I really was just a little tipsy.

The tiny apartment consisted of a living room and a comfortable bedroom, with a bathroom in between. The balcony in the back looked into the thick tropical foliage that rimmed the property, which was about three blocks from the ocean. This was a trendy place to stay, and the bar could get interesting some nights.

Marty took a look around the place and turned to face me. "We could use some music," he said with a slight slur to his words.

The next thing I knew, we were blasting an older Gloria Estefan song through the oversize external speakers for my iPhone. We also managed to make it to the bamboo-framed couch, and started to make out like teenagers. It was fun and I was getting swept up in it. I lost track of time until I heard a rap on the front door. It might've been going on for a while because it just sort of crept into my consciousness past the music and Marty's kisses.

Someone was now pounding on the door.

JAMES PATTERSON
BOOKSHOTS
OUT THIS MONTH

113 MINUTES

Molly Rourke's son has been murdered . . . and she knows who's responsible. Now she's taking the law into her own hands.

THE VERDICT

A billionaire businessman is on trial for violently attacking a woman in her bed. No one is prepared for the terrifying consequences of the verdict.

THE MATING SEASON

Sophie Castle has been given the opportunity of a lifetime: her own wildlife documentary. But her cameraman, Rigg Greensman, is unmotivated . . . and drop dead gorgeous.

TRUMP VS. CLINTON: IN THEIR OWN WORDS (ebook only)

Direct from the candidates, *Trump vs. Clinton* is an unvarnished conversation on the issues in this dramatic presidential election.

JAMES PATTERSON BOOKSHOTS

COMING SOON

FRENCH KISS

French detective Luc Moncrief joined the NYPD for a fresh start – but someone wants to make his first big case his last.

$10,000,000 MARRIAGE PROPOSAL

A billboard offering $10 million to get married intrigues three single women in LA. But who is Mr. Right . . . and is he the perfect match for the lucky winner?

SACKING THE QUARTERBACK

Attorney Melissa St. James wins every case. Now, when she's up against football superstar Grayson Knight, her heart is on the line, too.

KILL OR BE KILLED

Four gripping thrillers – one killer collection. *The Trial, Little Black Dress, Heist* and *The Women's War*.

THE WOMEN'S WAR (ebook only)

Former Marine Corps colonel Amanda Collins and her lethal team of women warriors have vowed to avenge her family's murder.

BOOK**SHOTS**

STORIES AT THE SPEED OF LIFE

www.bookshots.com

ALSO BY JAMES PATTERSON

Private Down Under (*with Michael White*)
Private L.A. (*with Mark Sullivan*)
Private India (*with Ashwin Sanghi*)
Private Vegas (*with Maxine Paetro*)
Private Sydney (*with Kathryn Fox*)
Private Paris (*with Mark Sullivan*)
The Games (*with Mark Sullivan*)

NYPD RED SERIES

NYPD Red (*with Marshall Karp*)
NYPD Red 2 (*with Marshall Karp*)
NYPD Red 3 (*with Marshall Karp*)
NYPD Red 4 (*with Marshall Karp*)

STAND-ALONE THRILLERS

Sail (*with Howard Roughan*)
Swimsuit (*with Maxine Paetro*)
Don't Blink (*with Howard Roughan*)
Postcard Killers (*with Liza Marklund*)
Toys (*with Neil McMahon*)
Now You See Her (*with Michael Ledwidge*)
Kill Me If You Can (*with Marshall Karp*)
Guilty Wives (*with David Ellis*)
Zoo (*with Michael Ledwidge*)
Second Honeymoon (*with Howard Roughan*)
Mistress (*with David Ellis*)
Invisible (*with David Ellis*)
The Thomas Berryman Number
Truth or Die (*with Howard Roughan*)
Murder House (*with David Ellis*)
Never Never (*with Candice Fox*)

NON-FICTION

Torn Apart (*with Hal and Cory Friedman*)
The Murder of King Tut (*with Martin Dugard*)

ROMANCE

Sundays at Tiffany's (*with Gabrielle Charbonnet*)
The Christmas Wedding (*with Richard DiLallo*)
First Love (*with Emily Raymond*)

OTHER TITLES

Miracle at Augusta (*with Peter de Jonge*)

BOOKSHOTS

Black & Blue (*with Candice Fox*)
Break Point (*with Lee Stone*)
Cross Kill
Private Royals (*with Rees Jones*)
The Hostage (*with Robert Gold*)
Zoo 2 (*with Max DiLallo*)
Heist (*with Rees Jones*)
Hunted (*with Andrew Holmes*)
Airport: Code Red (*with Michael White*)
The Trial (*with Maxine Paetro*)
Little Black Dress (*with Emily Raymond*)
Chase (*with Michael Ledwidge*)
Let's Play Make-Believe (*with James O. Born*)
Dead Heat (*with Lee Stone*)
Triple Threat